"How many men have you kissed, Liv?"

"Enough. Ask anyone." The pulse in her throat fluttered frantically. "Unlike you, I don't have a reputation for not being much in the kissing department."

That was a semidesperate attempt to create a diversion, but Brady was intrigued, in the mood to push the advantage. And he couldn't stop looking at her mouth.

"I've never had any complaints about my technique. You shouldn't believe rumors."

"That's hard to do without any contradicting data...." She shrugged, but it was uneasy, not the nonchalant gesture she was going for.

"Well, then, with my reputation on the line, I feel obligated to provide you with the necessary information to prove myself."

Her mouth dropped open, and Brady forgot about his reputation and everything else except the need to taste her lips. He closed the distance between them and pulled her close.

"Here goes."

* * *

**The Bachelors of Blackwater Lake:
They won't be single for long!**

Dear Reader,

I'm often asked how I choose names for the characters in my books. The answer is that no name starts with the same letter in order to avoid confusion for the reader. After that, I simply pick ones I like that, in my mind, fit a certain personality. Sometimes the choice will be made in plot group.

Twice a year I meet with three writer friends for food, fun and plotting help. After all, four imaginations are better than one. Inevitably during a session there's a name—male or female— that becomes the universal one for secondary characters. With *One Night with the Boss*, the name was Leonard. So, when it came time for heroine Olivia Lawson to name her pretend boyfriend, I thought, *Why not Leonard?*

It was a lot of fun creating a character who never appeared "on screen" but profoundly affected the hero's perception of the woman he'd known for so long and finally admitted he loved. I hope you enjoy reading Brady, Olivia and, yes, Leonard's story as much as I enjoyed writing it.

Best,

Teresa Southwick

One Night with the Boss

—

Teresa Southwick

HARLEQUIN® SPECIAL EDITION®

Recycling programs
for this product may
not exist in your area.

ISBN-13: 978-0-373-65808-4

ONE NIGHT WITH THE BOSS

Copyright © 2014 by Teresa Southwick

Printed in U.S.A.

TERESA SOUTHWICK

lives with her husband in Las Vegas, the city that reinvents itself every day. An avid fan of romance novels, she is delighted to be living out her dream of writing for Harlequin.

To Claudia Haugh Stepan
with thanks for being my friend.

Chapter One

Olivia Lawson would rather walk naked in a hailstorm than say what she had to say to her boss.

Again.

She hesitated outside his office—which also happened to be in his house, because it was a really big house. Brady O'Keefe owned and headed an internet conglomerate and, except for her, all of his one hundred plus employees worked remotely from leased office spaces in L.A., Chicago, New York and Austin. He managed everything effortlessly from his six-thousand-square-foot command center in a very exclusive, very upscale housing development in Blackwater Lake, Montana.

Her parents still lived in the house where she'd grown up, several doors down from the O'Keefes. She'd known Brady since they were kids and had worked as his administrative assistant for the last five years. Delivering the news that the professional relationship was about to end wouldn't be easy. She knew that because she'd tried to do it twice before.

As much as she loved her job, and dare she say it, cared for her boss, she had to make a break. She saw Brady not as her boss, but as a man. A handsome, charming, intelligent man. The problem was, he hadn't noticed her as a woman. As far as Brady was concerned she could be a piece of office furniture. She was as necessary as a computer, desk or stapler. The reality had finally hit her that this wasn't going to change and unless she wanted to end up a spinster with too many cats, she had to leave.

His door was open, so she knocked on the frame of the doorway separating their offices and heard the usual grunt that meant she should come in. He was at the familiar spot behind his L-shaped desk, staring at the computer screen. His back was to her and, as always, he didn't look up.

"Brady, I need to talk to you." His focus was extraordinary and normally she was awed by it. Not today. "There's a fire in the kitchen and I called nine-one-one."

"Uh-huh."

In the spirit of today, this was the first day of the rest of her life; today was the day she was going to tell him that everything was going to change. But she couldn't do that until he was listening. Time to get creative.

She walked over to his desk and picked up the orange foam rubber ball that he squeezed when deep in thought. After crushing it in her palm, she threw it at his head. Hard.

He glanced over his shoulder. "The kitchen's not really on fire, is it?"

"So you heard me."

"I always do."

If only that were true. "There's something I have to tell you."

"I guess it's important enough to hurl spheres at me." He slid his chair away from the computer, swiveled and faced her. Then he picked up the orange ball that had landed on his desk. Squeezing it he said, "Okay. You have my undivided attention."

Since turning fifteen years old, she'd wondered how it would feel to have all his concentration focused on her. This token of his interest wasn't what she'd had in mind, but sadly, it was all she would ever know. And that wasn't enough for her. But this was a poor substitute. She had to get away before her spirit shriveled and disappeared.

"I'm giving my notice."

"Of what?"

For a smart guy, he could be irritatingly dense. Or he was deliberately deflecting, hoping to get her off message. Not this time. This time was going to be different.

"I'm tendering my resignation."

"You're leaving me? There's nothing tender about that."

"Not you." That was a lie of self-protection. No way could she tell him how right he actually was. "I'm leaving your company."

"You're abandoning me?"

"You're so melodramatic. Not everything is about you."

He squeezed the orange ball until his knuckles turned white. "Didn't we just go through this?"

"Not just."

"Same time last year."

"Pretty close," she allowed.

It was exactly the same time. There was something about being a few weeks into a new year that made a person want to change their life. And she should have known better than anyone that this man would remember, because he had a mind like a steel trap.

Not to mention a face and body that could make him a

model or movie star instead of the megasuccessful businessman he was. Dark brown hair, short and carelessly mussed, complemented the scruff on his cheeks and jaw. He probably hadn't shaved because he didn't have to. There were no outside meetings today. No hot date later. Since she kept his calendar, she knew about things like that.

He certainly wasn't trying to impress her. She thought he looked amazing no matter what. Not that he cared.

Olivia secretly sighed over the scruff—and everything else about her boss. *Piercing* was the only way to describe his green eyes, which snapped with intelligence and wicked humor. The casual white cotton shirt and worn jeans perfectly showcased his broad shoulders, muscular chest and flat abdomen that were the result of disciplined workouts on the state-of-the-art equipment in his upstairs gym. He could be *People* magazine's sexiest CEO and most eligible bachelor.

She would miss the view when she was gone, but sacrifices had to be made for the greater good.

"Okay." He nodded as if he'd made up his mind. "Based on past data from this time last year, giving notice is your way of asking for a raise."

"Not really." When she tried to quit last year, he'd offered her more money, but that wasn't why she'd stayed.

"Let's call it a cost-of-living increase. When you do the paperwork, give yourself however much you think is reasonable." The right corner of his mouth quirked up, unleashing a rogue dimple.

Damn that dimple. It opened the incredibly insubstantial door that was holding back all her insecurity and weakness. *Determination, don't desert me now,* she silently begged.

"What if I think the majority share of the company is a reasonable increase?" she asked.

"You don't."

"How do you know?"

"There's not an unfair or dishonest bone in your body."

So, he'd taken note of her bones. Should she be flattered? Just thinking that made her pathetic. "You can't be sure I haven't turned demanding and greedy."

"I'm willing to risk it."

The grin punctuating his words was proof that he saw her as a Goody Two-shoes. Wow, warm fuzzy from that. *Back on task.* "I'm not here for a raise. I just want to resign."

"No, you don't."

"Yes, I do," she said firmly. "Giving notice is the courteous thing to do when one is leaving one's employer."

The smile curving his mouth disappeared and those green eyes narrowed, as if he'd finally noticed something different this time. "You can't be serious about leaving."

"Sure I can."

"Well, I don't accept your resignation."

"You don't have a choice."

"The hell I don't," he said stubbornly.

"That's up to you." She slid her hands into the pockets of her slacks to hide the shaking. "But you're on notice that two weeks from now I'm not showing up."

He stood and walked around the desk. This was the part she dreaded, the part where he invaded her personal space without any clue how his blatant masculinity threatened to chase off her determination.

She turned away and concentrated on the fireplace, where wood was burning and crackling. The fire, the furniture, the man—everything—made a person feel warm and cozy inside as a dreary rain soaked the world on the other side of the window.

"Two weeks' notice is all you're giving me?"

"It's standard." She turned to face him.

"I can't find a replacement in that short a time. You need to give me a month. Two would be better."

She shook her head. "I know you, Brady. If I don't give you a deadline, you won't even look for anyone."

"I don't have time. You know that."

"So you better get cracking on my replacement." She turned away again, because the look on his face showed it was starting to sink in that she was completely serious this time. Feeling sorry for him was a luxury she couldn't afford.

"Don't do this, Liv."

The nickname chipped away at her defenses, weakened her resolve. "I have to."

"Why now? Nothing's changed in your life."

She whirled around to look at him. "How do you know?"

"I just do."

It was his cocky confidence that had anger coiling in her belly. The smug expression in his eyes conveyed his utter belief that her world revolved around him and he was very nearly right about that. Twice before she'd caved after giving notice, and if she didn't have anything to fight back with she'd cave this time, too.

She could barely breathe, almost as though she needed an oxygen mask, which was why she blurted out the first thing that popped into her mind.

"You're wrong, Brady. Something in my life has changed, and it's big." She looked him straight in the eye and told the biggest lie ever. "I met a man and I've fallen in love. I'm moving away from Blackwater Lake to be with him."

There was some satisfaction in the fact that he was sincerely shocked. "You're leaving town?"

That's what got his attention? Not the fact that she was in love? "Yes. For a man."

She felt compelled to add that last part in case there was any question.

"Where did you meet this man?" His tone was neither suspicious nor curious. Mostly he sounded irritated.

Clearly Olivia hadn't thought through the made-up boyfriend exit strategy. It never crossed her mind that Brady would ask questions, and she wasn't particularly good at spontaneous deceit.

"It's none of your business."

He folded his arms over his chest and stared her down. "I couldn't disagree more. You're not just a valued employee, you're…"

"What?"

"My friend."

Olivia made sure the expression on her face didn't change. For just a second she'd felt hope that he might think of her as *more*. After five years of not being more it was silly, foolish and stupid to be disappointed, but none of that stopped her. Still, she was determined that he wouldn't know, not even by the barest flicker of an eyelash.

"You're my boss," she corrected him. "That's all. Our working relationship doesn't entitle you to information about my personal life."

"I just asked where you met him. How is that personal?"

"It's prying."

"I'm curious. So take me out back and flog me."

"Tempting," she said. "But it's raining and I don't want to get my hair wet."

"Oh? Do you have a hot webcam date?" She gave him a look and he held up his hands. "The least you can do is tell me his name."

"Again—prying."

"Are you ashamed of him? Ichabod? Aristotle? Sven?" He tapped his lip thoughtfully. "Maybe it's a girl name. Lindsay? Lynne? Carroll?"

She almost laughed, almost succumbed to the charm. Instead, she decided to run for cover. She turned away and headed for the door. "You're incorrigible and listening to this isn't in my job description."

"Why can't he move here to Blackwater Lake?"

Because he doesn't exist, she thought. "It's just easier if I go there." That was sort of true.

"Easier on who?"

"Me."

"So where are you moving?"

"Again—prying. Look, I did what I had to do. You've got your two weeks' notice. Now I'm going back to work. There are a lot of loose ends to tie up."

Behind her he said, "Most administrative assistants would be eager to give their boss all the juicy, gossipy details of a love affair."

"I'm not most assistants."

"Tell me about it." He sounded like a petulant little boy, pouting about not getting his way.

That should have reinforced her decision, but as always, she found the behavior oddly endearing.

She stood in the doorway between their offices. "So, I'll advertise my position and hopefully you can promote from within the company. I'll also contact an employment agency and recruiters we've used in the past. I'll work over the weekend and on Monday there will be a slate of candidates for you to interview."

"Whatever."

Olivia closed the door, then walked over to her desk and sat behind it. She let out a long breath and realized the last few minutes in Brady's office were just a preview of what she could expect from him for the next two weeks. Giving him her resignation was a walk in the park compared to the prospect of actually working with him every day until she left.

He wasn't going to make this easy on her.

Three days after Olivia had given her notice, Brady leaned back in his desk chair and squeezed the orange ball. It was Monday and she'd kept her word about lining up people for her job. He'd just completed the second of two interviews she'd scheduled for today and she was seeing the applicant out.

"Olivia must be really anxious to get out of here," he said to himself, crushing the round foam rubber in his palm.

Who was this guy she'd met?

He'd never thought about her dating, let alone getting serious. And he wasn't sure what bothered him more— losing the world's best assistant, or the fact that she was leaving because she'd fallen in love. He hated change— and the thought of her with a guy made him want to rip what's-his-name's head off.

The situation basically sucked.

He swiveled in his chair and looked out the big arched window. No rain today. It was beautiful outside, with the sun turning the surface of Blackwater Lake to sparkling diamonds. The other window had a view of the mountains and he knew that from her desk just a few feet away Olivia could look at the same beautiful surroundings.

Was there mind-blowing scenery where what's-his-name lived?

"So, what do you think about the interviews?"

Brady knew Olivia's voice, but he'd realized she was in his office before she'd said a word. The scent of her filled the room and always made him think of flowers. A garden. Serenity.

But not anymore. Now she was going to turn his life upside down to move somewhere he didn't know with a guy she wouldn't name.

He swiveled his chair around and looked at her. She was wearing a very businesslike, conservative navy pantsuit and matching pumps. Today her strawberry-blond hair was pulled away from her face in a ponytail, emphasizing her high cheekbones. Her big blue eyes filled with eager anticipation when she sat in one of the club chairs on the other side of his desk.

She wasn't tall and willowy or classically beautiful, but her smile always brightened the room on a cloudy day. And there was something about her voice, a huskiness that wasn't quite a lisp but tapped into his devilish streak and made him bait her into saying S-words.

She was staring at the rubber ball in his fist. "You've clearly been giving the interviews some thought."

"Sort of. In a manner of speaking. But only because you forced me into this."

She rolled her eyes, then looked at the yellow legal pad in her lap that she used for notes. "Okay, then. Let's start with candidate number one. Shannen Dow."

The corners of his mouth curved up. "I like her name."

"That's a good start. The recruiter says she's one of their strongest applicants."

"Of course they would. Commission is their revenue stream."

Olivia ignored that. "I thought she was very bright, with a solid background in computers and business. That's really important so she can hit the ground running. The sooner you hire someone, the more training I can do before my last day."

The *last day* part hit a nerve. "She was okay. But it has to be said—not a fashion plate."

Her blue eyes narrowed on him. "I didn't list accessorizing as a qualification you were looking for. Since when do you care about that?"

"Since always. She'll have to meet clients and there will be meetings."

"Not often. When I interviewed, you told me that since your corporate office is in your home, I could wear jeans to work."

Because jeans look good on you, he thought. But Shannen Dow was skinny and her voice wasn't the least bit gravelly or interesting.

"But you never did go casual and that's set a very high bar for your replacement."

"So take her to the mall."

Brady ignored the sarcasm. "Didn't you find the tone of her voice to be like fingernails on a chalkboard?"

Olivia's expression was wry. "Not until you asked her to make a pot of coffee."

"Really? I thought the pitch was on the shrill side. Too much of that would give me a headache."

"No one wants to work for a male sexist pig," she pointed out.

"She needed to know I'm missing the sensitivity chip," he defended.

"Making coffee isn't a skills requirement for this position."

"Says who? It's important to me and I'm the one who signs the paycheck."

"Okay then. Moving on." She made a note on the legal pad. "Let's talk about candidate number two."

"What's her name again?" he asked innocently.

"Shelly Shows." She met his gaze. "Did you approve of her outfit?"

"It was lovely." He added, "But I wasn't wowed by her, even in plaid."

"Her letters of reference are glowing. At her current place of employment she's very well-liked and efficient."

"Then why does she need this job?"

"It's closer to home. She's been working as executive assistant to the administrator of the hospital, which, as you're aware, is about seventy miles away. Currently she rents a room near work then comes home on the weekends." Olivia met his gaze. "So, what are your thoughts?"

He thought it would be possible to sympathize if the best assistant he'd ever had wasn't leaving him. Instead of answering, he asked, "Speaking of distant towns, where are you moving?"

She blinked at his rapid change of topic. "What?"

"When you abandon me, where are you going to live?"

"That's not information you need in order to hire my replacement."

Why was she being so stingy with details? "The least you can do is tell me his name."

"You're not going to let this go, are you?"

He leaned back in his chair and grinned. "See how well you know me?"

"All right. It's Leonard," she finally said. "There, go ahead and make fun."

"Would I do that?"

"In a heartbeat."

"That's harsh." But accurate. He'd almost said it was marginally better than Aloysius. "So, where did you meet Leonard?"

"Out of town," she said vaguely.

"That goes without saying. If you were dating a guy from Blackwater Lake, it would be all over town." For a to-the-point person, she was being uncharacteristically difficult. This was frustrating and Brady felt his curiosity picking up momentum. "Where specifically did you meet? On vacation?"

"Vacation?" She laughed. "What's that? When you're in the office I am, too. And you're always in the office. There's no such thing as time off."

"Point taken. I'm a workaholic. Would you consider a leave of absence instead of resigning? I could spare you for that."

"No." Primly she folded her hands in her lap. "Not everything is about you."

"So you keep reminding me. And now it's about Leonard."

"Exactly." She brushed imaginary lint from the leg of her slacks.

"If you didn't meet him on vacation, it must have been a trip for work."

"Remind me not to try and put anything over on you."

Sarcasm was one of his favorite things about her. "So, was it in Austin? L.A.? Chicago?"

"I definitely went to those cities. You should know. We were there together."

She was right about that, but when business hours were over they'd gone their separate ways. He'd picked up women and if Olivia had met men she never said anything to him. Until now. He'd never thought to ask how she filled her time away from work. Clearly she'd found Leonard, and the sense of betrayal Brady felt was out of proportion to the situation. He was being unfair. Not to mention completely irrational.

As crazy as he knew it was, he wanted to know everything. "Do you have a job lined up in Leonard's neck of the woods?"

"I have an offer."

"I'd be happy to give you a glowing recommendation." Well, not happy, exactly, but he'd try not to be spiteful, what with his festering bitterness about her jumping ship.

"But I'm planning to take some time off first."

"What are you going to do with yourself?"

"Anything that strikes my fancy," she said, a little defiantly. She stood and walked to the doorway of his office. "Any other questions?"

Why are you leaving me?

Brady didn't say that out loud, even though the idea of it had preoccupied him way too much since she'd dropped her bombshell. Besides his mother, sister and niece, he had no personal attachments—yet somehow he'd become attached to Olivia. He wouldn't be making that mistake with his next assistant.

She looked over her shoulder on the way out the door. "Think about Shelly. And I'll be lining up more candidates to interview. If you know what's good for you, you'll approach this process more seriously than you just did."

"I conducted those interviews very seriously."

She ignored that. "You need to ask yourself what's wrong with the two women you saw today."

"I don't need to ask myself anything. I already know what's wrong."

"Care to share?" She put a hand on her hip.

"Neither of them is you."

Chapter Two

After work, her boss's words sent Olivia to her best friend's house. A friend who just happened to be Brady's sister. Now she sat on Maggie Potter's comfortable sofa in the cozy, spacious log cabin home where Maggie lived with her infant daughter, Danielle, after her husband was tragically killed in Afghanistan. Danny had built this place for her and it was where they'd planned to spend the rest of their lives and raise their family. That was before his Army National Guard unit had been called up and deployed to Afghanistan, where he was killed by a roadside bomb, leaving his pregnant wife a heartbroken widow.

Maggie was a petite brunette with big brown eyes that now always seemed a little sad. After Danny's death Olivia had tried to be there for her friend as much as possible and had insisted on a weekly girls' night out. After baby Danielle was born, Olivia brought dinner to the house so the little girl wasn't left out of the female ritual. But tonight the toddler had gone to bed early, worn out from a play date.

Olivia scooted forward and took her glass of Merlot from the coffee table where it sat by the pizza box. "I have something to tell you," she said.

"Gossip?" Maggie's brown eyes gleamed with undisguised feminine interest. "Please tell me it's juicy. There hasn't been any good buzz since Emma Robbins came to town, got a job as nanny to Justin Flint's little boy, then announced she was the long-lost daughter of Michelle and Alan Crawford."

Olivia grinned, remembering the sensational events. "Don't forget the part where she and Justin fell in love and are now engaged to be married."

"I couldn't have said it better." Maggie put her paper plate with the half-eaten slice of pizza on the ottoman in front of her. "So, what's the scoop?"

"This isn't gossip or even buzz. If you haven't heard about it already, you will soon and this news should come from me."

"You're not sick, are you?"

"No." She hadn't meant to be so melodramatic. This woman had lost the love of her life and didn't need another scare. "I've never felt better. Have you talked to your brother?"

"Not for a few days." The frown eased, but only a little. "Just spit it out. What's going on and how is Brady involved?"

"I gave him my notice. I'm quitting and moving away from Blackwater Lake."

Maggie looked shocked, but not alarmed. "Where are you going?"

"California. A friend from college is going to start a tech business and offered me an upper management job."

"I see." Maggie smiled sadly. "So you're really going to quit this time?"

"Third time is the charm." Olivia wasn't sure she could pull off a this-is-good-news face, so she took a sip of wine instead.

"What makes you think Brady can't talk you into staying? Just saying…past history and all."

Cradling her wineglass in her hands, Olivia said, "That's the thing. I didn't plan to say it. The words just slipped out."

"What words?"

"He was so smug. So confident that I didn't mean what I said."

Maggie's full lips curved up. "So, my brother's management style remains exactly the same and he's taking you for granted."

Maybe it was guilt about the lie, but Olivia felt compelled to defend him. "He's a really good boss. Generous compensation and a comprehensive benefits package for his employees. Bonuses. Working conditions are good."

"And yet you're determined to leave," her friend pointed out, looking puzzled.

"I have to."

Olivia shared everything with Maggie—except about Brady. Once after a night out with Sydney McKnight she'd had her friend drop her at Brady's house and had every intention of confessing that she cared for him. Two glasses of wine later, she'd fallen asleep on his couch without spilling the beans. Later, she'd realized that was for the best. If he couldn't return her feelings honestly, she didn't want him to know how she felt.

Maggie sat forward in the chair. "So, what were the words that just slipped out?"

Olivia met the other woman's gaze. "I told Brady I met

a man, fell in love and I'm quitting. That I have to move away to be with him."

"Wow, that's a pretty big lie. I hope it wasn't National Honesty Day or anything."

"Me, too. That would probably send me deeper into the pit of hell than I already am." Olivia took another sip of wine. "I feel awful about it, Mags, but like you said, he has this way about him. Some kind of powerful charisma that completely obliterates a person's will even when they'd made up their mind about the best thing to do."

"A person." Maggie slid back and tucked her legs up beside her in the chair. "Hmm…"

"What does that mean?"

Instead of answering the question, Maggie said, "Did you notice that I never asked *why* you're leaving Brady?"

It must be a sibling thing, she thought, remembering his all-about-me response to her two weeks' notice. "I'm not leaving *him.* I just won't be working for his company any more."

"Okay." Maggie used her exaggeratedly patient voice. "I didn't ask before, but I am now. Why did you quit?"

"It's time. This job offer came up…" She shrugged.

"Maybe it's because you have feelings for him."

"Of course I do," she said, trying to make light of it. "He's a terrific boss. And sort of like an honorary brother, through my association with you."

"That's not what I meant and you know it," Maggie scolded. "You think I don't see the way you look at him when you think no one's watching? A woman who's known that feeling can easily see it in someone else."

Olivia recognized the knowing expression in her friend's eyes. "You never said a word."

She lifted a shoulder. "It's your business. As your good

friend, I stood ready to help if and when you wanted to talk about it."

"I wanted to tell you." She reached over and squeezed her friend's hand. "But I was afraid it would put you in the middle and didn't want to chance that Brady would find out. You wouldn't mean to say anything, but stuff has a way of slipping out. Then things get awkward. If you didn't know, everyone is protected."

"Everyone but you, Liv."

"So you and I are okay?"

"Of course. Pinkie swear."

Olivia held up the correct finger and hooked her friend's. "Thanks, Mags."

"Don't mention it. I'm on your side. I know that you haven't been happy lately."

"Is it that obvious?"

"Only to me. My brother is oblivious and charming in equal parts. He also has this annoying habit of getting everything to go his way. I'm not at all surprised you made up a boyfriend as a way out."

"You're not?"

Maggie shook her head. "A self-made man as prosperous as my brother didn't get where he is without being determined. And having good people around him."

As Olivia was one of his people, she said, "Thank you."

"You're welcome. He also doesn't like change and will do anything he can to prevent it."

"No kidding. Today he interviewed several women who applied for my job and found deal-breaking flaws in all of them."

"Because he doesn't want to lose you."

Olivia nodded. She knew she was good at her job. "The only reason he could come up with for not hiring either of the qualified applicants was that none of them were me."

"Wow." Maggie's eyebrows rose. "So he does care."

"It wasn't personal." But the words had had her heart going for a minute. Then reality had set in and she remembered the last five years of impersonal behavior. He was always friendly, but never asked her to dinner or a movie. There was never even a flicker of awareness or any sign that he'd wanted to kiss her. It was time to face reality. She had feelings for her boss that wouldn't stop and the only way to go after the life she wanted was to ditch the job.

"I don't think he believes that I'm serious about quitting," Olivia said.

"So you had to do what you had to do."

"Yes." She sighed. "I hope you know that I'm not normally a liar."

"You're the most honest, straightforward person I know." Maggie smiled.

"Thanks for understanding."

"I understand more than you know. It's not easy to let go." Maggie glanced at a framed picture sitting on the end table beside her. The Tiffany lamp highlighted her handsome, smiling husband in his camouflage uniform and her eyes filled with a wistful, sad expression. "This isn't making excuses for my brother, but you know that he took our father's death pretty hard."

"Who wouldn't? I can't even imagine losing my father."

Maggie's remote expression indicated she was remembering. "Brady had just gotten home from college for Christmas break and we were all looking forward to being together for the holidays. Dad had a heart attack and literally died in his arms."

"I remember."

"He was different after that. More aloof. Driven." She shrugged.

Olivia hadn't really seen that much of him then. They

never talked or hung out and he went back to school. She only knew the now Brady, and he showed no sign of ever seeing her the way she wanted him to.

"He is the way he is, Mags, and I finally realized this isn't about him. It's about me and my life. If I don't make the break now, I never will."

"True enough. So, not only do I get why you fibbed, I will help you pull this off. I'll back up your story."

"You will?"

"Absolutely." She raised her arm and curled her fingers into her palm. "Girl power."

Olivia bumped her fist. "Females unite."

"Brady will ask me about this and I'll tell him how deliriously happy you are with...does he have a name?"

"Leonard."

"Really?" Maggie's lips twisted as if she'd sucked a sour lemon. "Not Lance? Stone? Or Indiana Jones?"

"Like I said...didn't plan this. The falsehood was in no way premeditated or I would have come up with something romantic like...Jean Luc."

"Okay. Leonard it is." Maggie laughed, then turned serious. "Stay strong, Liv. Stick to your guns if it's what will make you happy."

Olivia wasn't sure about future happiness, but she knew for a fact she wasn't content now. The clock was ticking and she wasn't getting any younger. Doing nothing wasn't an option.

Ever since Olivia had left for the day, Brady had been battling the urge to go through her computer files and get more information on Leonard.

"The loser," he muttered.

She'd left him no choice what with her tight-lipped lack of details. He was hurt, really. They were better friends than this. He would give her data about a woman if he got serious. Then again, he made it a point not to get serious.

Olivia was different. She deserved all the best things that life had to offer and it was incumbent upon him as her boss, *and friend,* to find out about this guy and make sure he was on the up-and-up.

Like a dieter looking at a seven-layer death-by-chocolate cake, he paced back and forth in her office, fighting the itch to search her files for Leonard-related information.

"What can it hurt? Who will know?" When his damned annoying conscience pointed out that he was better than this, he said out loud and with self-righteous defiance, "No, I'm not."

He sat in her chair and hit the power button, then waited impatiently for the machine to boot up. It seemed to take forever. She should have told him she needed a faster computer. This was a waste of time and money. Finally it was ready and he clicked on the first file, which was data on her out-of-town trips. Where she'd met Leonard.

"The loser."

She kept copious notes on everything work-related and her travel was no exception. He'd hoped to hit pay dirt right away, because the less time he spent digging, the less dirty he would feel. A man had to cover his backside, too. On the off chance his poking around was found out, there was plausible deniability. She wasn't here; he needed a file. It was his story and he was sticking to it. But he was getting frustrated. Everything he saw was budgets, meetings, cost projections and troubleshooting.

The next step was her email, if he decided to go there. It wasn't an easy choice, because that crossed into her personal life. Although now he knew that was probably where information on Leonard would be found. None of his business. Then again, she'd quit for personal reasons and was leaving him. That kind of made it his business.

"Okay, then. My motivation is quantified." He clicked on her work email, which was password protected.

In case he ever needed files, she'd given him her core code word and the system she used to change it, one she could remember: her mother's maiden name with the number of the current month and year. This was January, so he hit the one key, and it was an even-numbered year, so he entered it after *Clark*. In an odd-numbered year, it would have been before the name.

"I'm in," he said triumphantly, even as he felt his conscience protest.

Patting himself on the back seemed a little excessive, since it wasn't even a challenge. There was nothing the least bit stealthy or surreptitious about Olivia. She was open and honest, completely incapable of seeing the dark side to people. Otherwise she'd have seen Brady's dark soul a long time ago. That also meant she couldn't see anything bad in Leonard if it was there, which was why he was scanning her emails.

"Hmm. That's weird."

"What would that be?"

He looked up and Olivia was standing in the doorway. *Crap and double crap,* he thought. What would James Bond do in a situation like this?

Charm his way out of it.

"Olivia." He stood up and gave her the smile that had always kept his mother from taking away his computer when he was in teenage trouble. "You're looking especially lovely this evening."

"Really?" One of her perfectly shaped eyebrows lifted. "I look exactly the way I did all day and you never said a word about my appearance."

"Speaking of that…" He walked around her desk and assumed a casual pose, leaning a hip on the corner. "I didn't hear you come in."

"I used my key and the disarmed security system chirped the way it always does. You must have been really wrapped up in something."

"Ah." Since she came and went at will, she needed the system code to deactivate. And he had been oblivious to the sound of the front door opening. Time to shift focus. "I was very comfortable giving you a key. You see? That's how much I trust you. How can you expect the total stranger who replaces you to be entrusted with easy access to not only my home, but my company?"

Her purse strap slid down her arm and she readjusted it to her shoulder. "It's about time you built a corporate office for O'Keefe Technology, Inc. with state-of-the-art security."

She was right. He'd been talking about it for a while and had made up his mind to get the project started. The only reason he'd been dragging his feet was because that move would change everything—and he hated change.

"So, how is Maggie?"

"How did you know I saw your sister?"

Apparently helping himself to her computer made her suspicious about everything. "You told me you were leaving early to pick up a pizza to take over there."

"Right. I forgot." Wariness faded for a nanosecond before her eyes narrowed. "A slipup caused by the shock of finding you going through my computer."

"Oh, that." He glanced at it over his shoulder. "I was looking for your notes on the job applicants we saw today."

"I'm efficient, but not quite that good. I haven't input them yet. Why would you want anything that I might have jotted down?"

"Because I'm the boss."

He shrugged, but that was more about hiding the shudder those words produced. That response was the equivalent of a mother's final argument against a child who refused to take no for an answer. Plus her implied accusation was true and he needed something irrefutable to cancel out his devious behavior.

"You didn't like any of the women you interviewed," she pointed out.

"I might have been a tad harsh."

"You don't mean that." Her tone challenged him to deny it.

She knew him too well. It was both a blessing and a curse. Time to change the subject yet again. "So, what are you doing back here tonight?"

"There's some work I need to finish up and I forgot the file."

"Don't worry about that. It will keep until tomorrow."

She shook her head. "That's where you're wrong. I need to wrap up everything I can in the next week."

"And a half," he added.

"What?"

"It's a week and a half until your notice is up."

"What a relief." There was a touch of sarcasm in her tone. "And I thought there was nowhere near enough time to tie up a bazillion loose ends before my last day."

"I have complete faith in your ability to do that." Brady knew the file she wanted was on her desk behind him. But so was her email. So far he'd kept her from seeing it. "Go home and relax. I don't want to take advantage of you."

"Since when?"

"That's a cheap shot."

She sighed. "You're right. It's never been your management style to insist on overtime. This is my problem. I have a tendency to obsess about finishing up projects."

"So, I'm giving you a dispensation. Take the night off and don't think about the office."

"Very generous of you," she allowed. "But I feel an obligation to get as much done as possible for as long as I can." She moved closer and started to walk around the desk.

Without thinking it through, Brady suddenly stood in her path and she walked into him. She put her hands on his chest and looked up, her eyes opening wide.

His fingers automatically curved around her arms, urging her even closer. She was wearing a coat, but it was unbuttoned and he could feel her breasts pressed against him. The sweet scent of her skin invaded his senses and he had the most insane desire to wrap his arms around her and kiss her until they were both out of their minds. This wasn't the first time touching her had produced this reaction, but it was definitely stronger than ever before. Her full lips parted and there was a catch in her breathing that pointed toward her feeling the same kind of crazy he did.

She backed up a step and took a deep breath. "What is it you don't want me to see, Brady?"

Damn. There was that knowing-him-too-well thing again and this time it was the curse part. *Create a diversion.* "What makes you think that?"

"This is me. The innocent act doesn't work. You're up to something." She made a sudden move and side-stepped him.

She wasn't really that quick; he was simply that slow. It's what happened even to smart guys when blood flowed south of the belt. In the split second he'd been getting his breathing under control, Olivia was around the desk and staring at her computer monitor.

"This is my email." There was outrage in her tone.

"It is." What else could he say when caught red-handed? "But it's my computer."

"An employee has an expectation of privacy."

Again he needed a distraction. "Is there something in it you don't want me to see?"

"Of course not. But this is beneath you."

He should have listened to that annoying voice of his conscience when it said something similar. But it was the bruised and betrayed expression in her blue eyes that was his undoing. He couldn't stand it when she looked at him that way.

"Okay. You're right. I'm sorry. I shouldn't have done this."

"How could you?"

"In my defense, I want you to know that this is the first time. And it's kind of your fault."

"Oh, that's a good one. How do you figure?"

"If you hadn't been so stingy with details about Leonard…"

The glare instantly disappeared, replaced with an expression that was sheepish. Or guilty? "It's my business."

"So you said. But I'm concerned about you and what you're planning to do worries me. Because of my company," he amended.

"I don't know whether to be furious or flattered."

"Probably both."

"I'd warn you not to do it again, but you *are* the boss. My files are your files." She picked up the manila folder on her desk and met his gaze. "So what was weird?"

He realized she could teach him something about diversionary tactics. The question caught him off guard. "What?"

"When I walked in you were talking to yourself. Which,

by the way, is the definition of weird," she said. "But that's not what you meant. You were referring to my messages. So, what did you find that was weird?"

He shrugged as if to say he'd forgotten whatever it was that had brought those words to mind. "Whatever it was is gone now."

"Okay. And that's my cue. I'm gone, too." She turned and headed for the doorway. "See you in the morning, *boss*. And from now on I won't be doing email here."

"Okay." He deserved that. "Night, Liv."

She walked out faster than he'd thought those short but very lovely legs could go, obviously anxious to get away from him. Perversely, he realized that he was very much looking forward to seeing her tomorrow.

It had a lot to do with the fact that there was now a time limit on morning coffee with Olivia. Her warm smile when she asked how he was every day. The fragrance that she brought into the room with her, a chemical reaction created by her perfume interacting with her skin that made him acutely aware of her presence. Knowing why didn't make it any less potent when it happened.

But it wasn't going to happen very much longer, and he didn't like that one bit.

She had every right to be more furious than she'd been and that made him more curious, if possible. Brady glanced at the list of messages on the screen. There were some from her mom, dad and sister. Maggie had sent her a joke and a link to a cooking site. There was spam from shopping sites she'd browsed, but the weird factor hit him again.

"There's not a single thing from the man you quit your job for, Liv. What's up with Leonard?"

Chapter Three

At work the next morning, Olivia still couldn't believe what Brady had done, although they had a nontraditional working relationship and she'd shared messages with him before. And, being a liar herself, she couldn't afford to be sanctimonious and judgmental. Since she'd arrived an hour ago, the door to his office had been closed, and it was almost never closed. Maybe because she'd caught him in the act, he was sufficiently shamed into backing off.

One could hope. That way all she had to do was work out the remainder of her notice and the unfortunate incident would be behind her. There'd be no reason to speak about Leonard again.

What she had to do was put all her energy into finding her own replacement. Time was getting short and it wasn't fair to throw some poor, unsuspecting woman into the deep end of Brady's pool. So to speak.

Then a thought occurred to her. Her boss had found

fault with every female candidate he'd met so far. Maybe she should look more closely at male applicants. Olivia threw herself into the search and lost track of time as she browsed internet employment sites and dissected résumés.

When the sound of the opening front door and the subsequent security system chirp drifted to her, she glanced at her clock and realized almost two hours had slipped away. Knowing the visitor was probably Brady's mother or sister, both of whom had keys, she figured it was time for a break.

A few moments later Maureen O'Keefe appeared in the doorway with her fifteen-month-old granddaughter in her arms. "Hi, Olivia. How are you?"

"Great." She stood and walked around her desk, smiling at the toddler. "Hello, Miss Danielle. You're looking very pretty in your pink shirt and denim overalls."

The baby had dark hair and eyes like her mother and grandmother. But Maureen's short hair was shot with silver and done in a piecey style with the back flipped up in a saucy shape. She was taller than Olivia and looked trim and attractive in designer jeans, expensive brown leather boots and a trendy camel coat over her thick winter sweater.

"How are you, Maureen?"

"Could be better."

When the toddler held out her arms, Olivia took her. "Are you okay, baby girl? Why is your nana making that frowny face? You tell her that causes wrinkles."

"I have a very good reason to risk wrinkles with this face," the older woman said grimly. "Do you remember Tiffani Guthrie?"

Olivia would never forget the witch who'd dumped Brady when he left college just before finals in his senior year. Instead of supporting him, whatever his reasons might be, Tiffani with an *I* took up with a guy on his way to the Texas oil fields by way of Vegas, where, rumor had it, they married at the drive-through Elvis chapel.

"Brady's old girlfriend."

"Miss Fake Boobs and Big Hair." Maureen's voice dripped with loathing. "I was at the Grizzly Bear Diner this morning and heard from Cissy Johnson who was talking to Betty Cordoba who's a friend of Tiffani's cousin George. Word is that she's coming back to Blackwater Lake."

"No." Olivia couldn't believe she'd have the nerve to show her face back here after treating Brady so badly. She hugged the baby close. "Why would she do that?"

"No one is exactly sure. And this is just a guess from piecing together snippets of information," the other woman confided. "But we think she landed herself in a bad situation with that Texas wildcatter. We're speculating that she's coming here to look up her old boyfriend—her *wealthy* ex-boyfriend—who can get her out of the whole mess. Can you believe the nerve of that woman?"

"Yes." Olivia had never liked her.

She'd watched Brady and Tiffani together, hating the fact that she'd been born too late for him to notice her. She'd never figured out what Brady saw in the woman. Well, maybe the well-endowed bosom. Pretty face. Gorgeous red hair. But it was her attitude that was so infuriating. She'd had a way of making a person feel small and insignificant. Once she'd told wide-eyed high schooler Olivia not to hold her breath that Brady would ever give her a tumble. It had never occurred to Olivia that the feelings she thought buried inside were actually there on her face for the world to see. After that she'd worked very hard at making her expression neutral.

When the baby grew restless in her arms, Olivia handed

her over to her grandmother. "Maybe you're wrong and she's not coming here."

"Maybe. But Brady needs to be prepared. And so does every other bachelor in Blackwater Lake. What kind of mother would I be if I didn't warn him?"

"I see your point."

Olivia had never known this woman to interfere in her children's lives. She was always there with support, advice when asked, a shoulder to cry on when needed and babysitting when necessary. If she felt honor bound to share this rumor with her son, there was probably a very good reason.

"So, is Brady busy?" She settled Danielle on her hip.

"Always." But she had no idea what her boss was doing. "I can buzz him for you."

"In a minute." Maureen set little Danielle on her feet and she immediately squealed in a decibel level that would shatter glass. She toddled around Olivia's desk toward the closed door of her uncle's office. Small hands slapped on the door and a few seconds later it opened.

"Well, look who's here." He picked up his niece and held her high over his head until she laughed delightedly. "Hi, sweetie pie. Nice to see you, too, Mom."

"I hope you still feel that way when you hear what I came to say."

"Oh?"

"It will keep for a minute. I was just about to ask Olivia what's going on with her these days."

He walked over to them, holding the baby and looking so comfortable with the child that it tugged at Olivia's heart.

"I can't believe she hasn't told you the breaking news," he said.

"What? You're getting married?" Maureen's eyes grew wide. "You're pregnant."

"Do you know something I don't?" His gaze met Olivia's as his niece's chubby index finger toyed with the button at the collar of his white cotton shirt. "Is there something you need to tell me?"

"No!" It was pretty much impossible to get pregnant when you weren't having sex. Not that she planned to share that personal information.

"What's going on?" Maureen looked between the two of them, obviously sensing undercurrents.

"Olivia has a boyfriend and she's given notice that she's leaving O'Keefe Technology."

His mother looked more shocked than if a pregnancy had been confirmed. "What?"

"Yes," Brady continued. "She's going to abandon me."

"That's a tad melodramatic, but essentially true," Olivia defended. Also true was the need to shift attention from herself before she was forced to lie to his mother. "The problem is that Brady's showing more than a little resistance to hiring my replacement."

"I don't believe it." There was a puzzled expression on his mother's face.

"It's true," Olivia and Brady said together.

"That you're being difficult? It's a given." Maureen waved her hand dismissively. "I'm surprised your mother didn't say anything. We had breakfast together this morning and she never mentioned anything about you quitting. Or leaving town. Or even having a boyfriend."

There were questions in Brady's eyes when he said, "Olivia is very secretive about Leonard."

"That's your boyfriend's name?"

So much for not having to speak of Leonard ever again. And if Maureen reacted like her son and daughter, there would be a fair amount of teasing about the name. She braced herself and said, "Yes."

When the little girl squirmed in his arms, Brady set her on the rug and she toddled over to the wastebasket to explore.

"What kind of work does Leonard do?"

"Oh, this and that." For the first time in her life Olivia wished she'd practiced the art of deceit, because then she'd be better at it.

"This and that in what field?" Maureen persisted.

"Tech." That was sort of true. She worked in the industry and Leonard was a figment of her imagination, therefore a part of her. It was a stretch, but a case could be made.

"Way to go, Mom. That's more information than I've been able to get out of her."

"Not for lack of snooping," Olivia said pointedly. "The thing is, Maureen, this sort of information has a way of spreading around town and I just wasn't ready to talk about it yet."

"I've known your mother since you were a baby and she's never been able to keep a secret. The fact that she did now means you're holding something over her head. It must be *big*."

"Kind of." The other woman was assuming her mother knew all about this news, and it was less complicated not to correct the impression. Meaning she'd stooped to lying by omission. If she'd been Pinocchio, by now her nose would have grown long enough to put someone's eye out. *Mental note: call Mom ASAP.*

Maureen looked skeptical. "Are you sure about all this, sweetheart?"

"I've given it a lot of thought and this will be good for me." Finally, a question she could answer truthfully.

"Then I certainly wish you the best of luck and every happiness."

"What about the part where she's leaving me in the lurch?" Brady complained.

"You'll survive." She glanced at the baby, who had tipped over the wastebasket, and hurried to grab her up. "No, Danielle."

"I'm not so sure I will survive, Mom."

"Man up, sweetheart." She headed for his office. "Hiring someone to replace Olivia will seem like a walk in the park compared to the news I have for you."

He shot Olivia a questioning look and held out his hands in a what's-up gesture before following his mother into the office and closing the door.

Olivia blew out a long breath and sat in the chair behind her desk. "Oh, what a tangled web we weave when first we practice to deceive."

She glanced over her shoulder and realized this might be her only chance to call her mother before Maureen O'Keefe did. Good news and bad traveled fast in Blackwater Lake, the blessing and curse of a small town.

She picked up the phone and punched in her mother's number because this news—like the fact that she was moving away—should come from her.

Maureen's news about his old girlfriend was a piece of cake for Brady, compared to the interviews Olivia had arranged for the afternoon. He stared at the young man sitting across the desk from him, the one who wanted Olivia's job. He glanced at the name on the résumé again. Christopher Conway. Along with Olivia, he'd been chatting with the guy for about fifteen or twenty minutes. He was good-looking, articulate and had a sense of humor.

"So, Chris, you graduated from the University of Montana last year. Since then you've worked for a large retail chain. Doing what?"

"Workman's comp." The blond, blue-eyed applicant looked about twelve.

"Okay."

He looked at Olivia, who was sitting in the club chair beside the impossibly young kid and thought she looked maybe fifteen. Suddenly he felt old and tired and a little desperate. She'd tried to quit twice before but both times he'd been able to talk her into staying. They'd never gotten to the point of interviews for her job, let alone a second round of them.

On paper this kid looked good, if he checked out. He was moldable. Graduated top of his class with a double major in computer science and business. His current job wasn't in his chosen field, but he'd probably taken it out of necessity in bad economic times while scoping out something better.

It was actually pretty shrewd of Olivia to recruit a man for the position, and Brady was tempted to make Chris an offer. But his current assistant was still his first choice.

"I know what you're thinking, Mr. O'Keefe."

Brady sincerely doubted that. "What is it you think is on my mind?"

"That I'm too young and I don't have the experience. But I'm smart and a hard worker. If you give me a chance, I promise you won't be sorry."

Brady believed him. This kid reminded him of Henry. He still missed his best friend. The two of them had dreamed of starting this company together, but fate had other plans.

"Brady?" Olivia's voice grounded him in the present.

Of all the interviews he'd done, this guy was at the top of the list, but he hadn't quite thrown in the towel on letting his assistant get away. He was also a pretty good judge of character and talent and wouldn't let a smart up-and-comer get away either.

"Okay, Chris. I'll be in touch." He stood and held out his hand.

"Thanks for seeing me, Mr. O'Keefe."

"The pleasure is mine. I'm sure you've got a bright future ahead of you."

That must have been the right thing to say, because Olivia smiled at him as if he'd hung the moon. Her approval always made him feel like a better man than he was.

"I'll show you out, Chris."

For just a moment there was the slightest lisp in her voice and that made him smile as he watched the two leave the room. But he couldn't indulge himself for long, because when she came back the game would be on.

A few moments later, she walked back into the room and sat in the chair where she'd observed the interview. "So what do you think?"

Here goes round two, he thought.

He moved to the club chair side of his desk and rested a hip on the corner. Her knees were inches from his leg and she angled them away.

"Who are we talking about?" he asked.

"Who do you want to start with?"

Could be his imagination, but along with the lisp there was a breathless quality to her words. "You pick."

"How about candidate number one? Heather Fontaine." She glanced at her notes. "Good computer skills. Experience. Qualified. A good fit."

"Those were your impressions?"

"Yes."

"You didn't jot down anything about her attitude?"

"No." Her eyes narrowed and gone was any trace of

her approving smile. "I didn't notice anything about an attitude."

"Hmm."

"What does that mean?"

"I don't know. There was just…" He crossed his arms over his chest. "Something. Instinct, maybe. A sense that she could be difficult."

"Meaning she would stand up to you and not get steam-rollered?" One eyebrow lifted, a dare to challenge her assessment.

"In a job interview, I have a finite amount of time to form an impression about someone I'll be working with." He shrugged. "In that time with Heather, my impression became aware of attitude."

"Did it occur to you that she was trying to project confidence?"

"No." When there was no response, he figured she was waiting for more. "When I interviewed you, you had an air of confidence and competence without even a hint of attitude."

"I see. So, even though time is getting short, your attitude hasn't changed." Her full mouth pulled tight. "Okay. Number two. Annabel Brown."

"She seems like a perfectly nice young woman. The right skill set. Good résumé." Brady put a hint of doubt into his tone.

"Attitude?" Olivia called his doubt and raised him a whole lot of sarcasm.

"Not from her, but *you're* walking a little close to that line."

"So fire me," she challenged.

"I think I can handle it a little longer." Brady couldn't imagine *not* handling it. Liv was dipped in determination, but wielded it wisely and with a sense of humor. For whatever argument she chose to pull out her attitude, it always passed the level-of-importance test.

"So Annabel has everything you're looking for. I'll contact human resources and get them going to fast-track a job offer…"

"Hold on."

She looked up. "What?"

Was that impatience he heard? "I didn't say I wanted to hire her."

"Why wouldn't you?"

"There's something missing. A focus. Fire in the belly. It's hard to put into words."

"Ellie Hart recommended her. She works for one of Ellie's brothers at Hart Incorporated. That's the big time and they don't tolerate fools. Annabel knows what she's doing but wants to do it here in Blackwater Lake. What are you trying to say, Brady?"

"She seemed a little less than motivated. On the lazy side." He was making that part up.

"She's from Texas." Olivia stood and shoved her hands on her hips. If it was possible to breathe fire, she would have. "People from the South have a drawl. That doesn't mean they can't be forceful when necessary."

He loved it when she got riled up, and it made her crazy when he suddenly switched gears. As he was about to do. "You're right. I'm no doubt misjudging her, so we'll just chalk it up to lack of chemistry."

"Okay. So it's a no on Annabel." She blew out a breath. "What about Chris? So far he's the first one you promised to contact."

"I like him."

"There's a *but*."

"How do you know?"

"Chalk it up to a lot of years working for you." She met

his gaze. "Plus you had a funny expression on your face during the interview. What was that about?"

A feeling had come over him that he hadn't experienced for a long time. Survivor's guilt. Henry was dead and Brady was alive. In college they had been excited about a future in business together, then suddenly Henry had died and all those dreams disappeared with him. Brady had to carry on alone. It was a stark reminder that anyone he cared about could be gone in an instant.

Brady looked at Olivia's face, so familiar, so alive, and realized he didn't know what he'd do without her. At work, of course. And she was waiting for an answer to her question.

"Chris reminds me of someone I used to know in college."

"Henry Milton," she said. "I noticed the resemblance, too."

He nodded. The two of them had been inseparable all through school, always at each other's houses. "Chris is bright, enthusiastic and would be an asset to this company."

"I thought so, too. So I'll offer him my job."

"No." He straightened away from the desk and looked down at her. "He's too young and inexperienced and smart enough to realize it."

"He can learn. I did."

"The thing is that you and I learned together. He'd be stepping into a high-power situation." He shook his head. "No, I think his talents would be better utilized in research and development. Contact human resources and tell them to find something for him."

"Okay. He'll be an asset to this company. But that means we're back to square one."

"It would appear so."

"You're too damn cheerful, Brady." Her eyes flashed with frustration. "You do realize that in another week I'm leaving. Whether or not you've hired anyone to replace me. This isn't a joke and I wish you would stop treating it that way."

She was being incredibly stubborn about this, and he blamed Leonard. "Why do you have to go?"

"You know why."

"Don't you think it's incredibly selfish of Leonard to insist that you move away?"

"He's not insisting." She met his gaze as if she expected a challenge.

"Okay, then. Why doesn't he relocate from..." He waited for her to fill in the blank with a city or state and when she didn't, he was peeved. "He should be the one to move, find a job in Blackwater Lake."

She blinked up at him for several seconds. "It's a small town and there's nothing here that would utilize his particular skills," she said after some thought.

Brady recognized the expression on her face. It was the one she wore when she had to think fast, to come up with an explanation or particular spin. The truth shouldn't take that much effort.

"What particular skills does he have?"

Her chin lifted in that stubborn, familiar way, just before she got defiant. "Well, for one thing, he's a good kisser."

"Is that right?"

That might get him a volunteer job at the charity fundraiser kissing booth, but gainful employment was questionable. He was aware of the edge in his voice and the tight knot in his gut. It was the first time he'd thought about her actually kissing Leonard. Or in Leonard's bed.

A man touching her, any man. He didn't like any of the above, not even a little bit.

This sensation had all the characteristics of jealousy but he couldn't believe that's what it was and didn't care right this minute. He still had questions. Like...

Were there other men? Wouldn't he know if there were? Who were they and why hadn't he met them?

He hadn't known about Leonard and suddenly, with an intensity that surprised him, he wanted to know everything.

"How many men have you kissed, Liv?"

"That's none of your business." Annoyance and indignation looked really good on her.

"I'm making it my business. You've worked for me a long time and I don't know who you hang out with. You say Leonard is a good kisser. How many men have you kissed to compare him with?"

"Enough. Ask anyone." The pulse in her throat fluttered frantically. "Unlike you, I don't have a reputation for not being much in the kissing department."

That was a semidesperate attempt to create a diversion but Brady was intrigued, in the mood to push the advantage. And he couldn't stop looking at her mouth.

"I've never had any complaints about my technique. You shouldn't believe rumors."

"That's hard to do without any contradicting data..." She shrugged, but it was uneasy, not the nonchalant gesture she was going for.

"Well, then, with my reputation on the line, I feel obligated to provide you with the necessary information."

Her mouth dropped open and Brady forgot about his reputation and everything else except the need to taste her lips. He closed the distance between them in one step, then threaded his fingers into her silky hair with one hand and pulled her close with the other.

"Here goes."

Chapter Four

Olivia couldn't believe this was happening. She'd wondered forever how it would feel to be in Brady's arms, with their bodies pressed together from chest to knee. The reality was so much better than anything her imagination had cooked up.

If this was a dream, she never wanted to wake up.

For one thing, she hadn't thought about his fingers threaded through her hair and how exquisitely *romantic* that would feel. Or the intensity darkening his eyes. The expression did things to her insides, things she couldn't put into words because the feeling was simply AWESOME. All caps!

His mouth hadn't officially touched hers yet and it was already the best kiss she'd ever had, proving that it wasn't *how* you kissed, but whom.

"Liv," he whispered, brushing his thumb across her cheek and then her lips.

The touch had heat mixed with shivers racing over her shoulders and arms. *So near yet so far,* she thought as his warm breath caressed her lips. It taunted and teased and she'd already waited years for this. She was so over being passive. On tiptoe, she closed the infinitesimal distance between them and softly pressed her lips against his as she slid one arm around his waist and the other hand up to his chest.

His heart thundered beneath her palm, making her heart thunder, too. His mouth was soft and met her own just before his tongue lazily skimmed her bottom lip. The flash was like tissue paper igniting and threatened to make her go up in flames.

Worse, the touch made her *anticipate.* She wanted his hands to find their way to her breasts, to settle on her hips and slide possessively over her stomach.

He nibbled the corner of her mouth and worked his way across her cheek to her ear. When he took the lobe gently between his teeth, she nearly gasped from the delicious sensation, came close to dissolving in a puddle at his feet. The touch almost made her forget that he was her boss. He was simply a man—who made her ache for so much more.

Olivia wished that she'd been the one to pull away first, but that wasn't the way it went. The only small satisfaction she got was that Brady looked surprised. And his breathing was definitely not steady. With luck that would keep him from noticing that she was having a bit of trouble pulling enough air into her lungs. Or that she was quivering with reaction and wanted more.

"So…" He took a step back. "What's the verdict? Are the rumors true?"

She blinked up at him and the words sounded like a recording played back on slow speed. That was because her brain didn't have enough oxygen to process his question at more than a crawl. "What?"

"You know. The rumor that I'm not much in the kissing department?"

Olivia snapped to as surely as if he'd dumped ice-cold water over her head. Her mind kicked into high gear as she put a thoughtful expression on her face.

"I can't speak for your other women," she said, "but as kisses go, that was adequate."

"Really?"

"Yes." She tapped her index finger against lips still throbbing from the all-too-brief, way-above-adequate close encounter. "I think that's a fair assessment."

"Adequate?" He sounded shocked and annoyed in equal parts.

"Yes. It was nice. I think the rumor must have come from someone who had expectations of more."

Technically that was true because, she'd made it up when he started pressuring her about Leonard being the one to relocate. Where Brady was concerned, she couldn't quite suppress expectations. In her own defense, she'd had to think fast, something that was becoming a necessity of late.

"Adequate? Wow. I never thought I'd say this, but that makes me wish you'd said it was fine."

From that she guessed he hated it when a woman used less than glowing adjectives about his performance. She couldn't resist messing with him, just a little.

"That works too," she agreed. "It was fine."

He groaned. "You're killing me here, Liv."

"I didn't mean to offend your fragile male ego. I'm just trying to be honest."

And failing miserably. That kiss was so much better

than fine or adequate. It was truly spectacular and she would swear the earth moved.

"From now on, I think I'd rather you lie to me."

"I can do that." Better than he knew.

"Okay, then." Brady dragged his fingers through his hair. "Look, do you mind locking up? I'm going to see Maggie and my niece. It's been awhile and I want to spend a little more time with them."

The visit was on his schedule and Olivia looked at her watch. This was a little earlier than he usually left. Frankly, she could use some time alone to collect herself. "Of course. I have some work to finish, but I'll make sure everything is shut down and the alarm is on."

"Thanks." He moved past her on his way to the doorway.

"Yeah. Tell Maggie hi and have a good evening."

Over his shoulder he said, "See you tomorrow."

When he was gone, a wave of sadness broke over her as reality sank in. He wouldn't be saying that to her too many more times and she would miss it terribly.

Sighing, she shut down his computer. Just then her cell phone rang and the caller ID announced her mother. Her stomach knotted because they hadn't talked yet. She'd had to leave a message and now her mom was getting back to her.

She hit the send button. "Hi, Mom."

"Hey, Livvie. Sorry I didn't call you sooner, but your text said to call when I had time to talk. Even now I barely have a minute, but wanted to get back to you. What's up? Is everything okay?"

Without actually answering that question, she asked one of her own. "Have you seen Maureen O'Keefe?"

"Not since we had breakfast this morning. Why?"

"There's something I have to tell you, Mom. You're aware that I've been thinking of quitting my job."

"Of course. You already gave your notice twice and Brady talked you into staying."

"He has a way of doing that. But this time I made sure it will take."

"You quit?" There was barely a question mark in her mother's voice.

"Yes. I didn't tell you guys in advance this time because of the other two times it came to nothing. But I had to tell Brady I was leaving."

"Well, of course you did. He's the boss and will need to replace you."

"Exactly. But Maureen dropped by and he told her."

"So that's why you're sharing now. You wanted us to hear it from you."

"Partly. It's just that this time I wanted to make sure I went through with it. The thing is, Mom, I've accepted a job with a college friend of mine who's starting up a technology company in California."

There was a moment of silence, long enough to make Olivia hate herself for not delivering this information face-to-face. But she couldn't chance that the news would get back to her mother before she'd had an opportunity to say something.

Finally words filled the silence. "That sounds like an exciting opportunity, sweetie. It's good to shake things up."

"Speaking of that…" She took a breath. "Maureen will ask you about my boyfriend…"

"You're going out with someone? Have I met him?"

"I'm pretty sure you haven't." No one had. Not even Olivia.

"That's wonderful, honey." Her voice sounded rushed.

"Look, I'm so sorry. But I have to run. Are you still coming for dinner this weekend?"

"Of course."

"Good. You can tell us all about your news then. Bye. Love you."

"Okay, Mom. Love you."

She hit the end button, then looked around Brady's office as she was about to turn off the lights. Her gaze rested on the place where they'd stood when he kissed her. Memories of that perfect moment squeezed her heart.

Why did he kiss her now, when she was really leaving? It would be one more thing to miss when she was gone. And she had a bad feeling that no man's kiss would ever be quite as incredibly, deliciously adequate as Brady's had been.

On the drive out of Blackwater Lake to his sister's house, Brady still couldn't quite believe he'd kissed Olivia. He was used to being the smartest guy in the room, but what he'd done was colossally dumb. In fact it set a new and higher bar for dumbness. Thanks to probably the hottest kiss he'd ever had, it made him completely aware of his executive assistant in every way. Not only that, he couldn't stop thinking about how easy and natural it would have been to sweep her upstairs and into his bed. And he was still regretting that he hadn't, because there was no doubt in his mind that she'd have gone with him.

Since the day he'd hired her, he'd always been able to close off these thoughts, but kissing her opened the door and there was no way to shove the messy flood of feelings back inside. So he needed a distraction.

"And I know just the thing."

He turned off the main road into Maggie's driveway and up to the three-story log cabin set in a clearing surrounded by evergreen trees. The yard in front had grass bordered by bushes and flowers, which were not blooming in January. This place was like something out of a fairy tale and any second he expected the seven dwarfs to march out of the woods singing "Hi Ho."

Brady exited the low-slung sports car then jogged up the steps and knocked. A few seconds later the dead bolt clicked.

Maggie opened the door. "Hello, Uncle Brady."

"Ba-ay!" His niece, pretty in pink from head to toe, toddled over and grabbed her mother's leg.

"If it isn't Snow White and the littlest dwarf, Sunshine." He grabbed up the little girl and lifted her high in the air, where she giggled happily. "How are my two favorite girls?"

"Don't let Mom hear you say that."

"She knows I put her into a completely different category."

"Right." Maggie grinned. "You're still her favorite."

"And you're still bitter about that." He settled Danielle on his forearm and moved farther into the room.

"Always."

His sister was a beautiful woman, and that was a strictly impartial male observation. Shiny brown hair fell past her shoulders to the middle of her back and her eyes, depending on her mood, were warm like dark cocoa or cool and shaded like smooth brandy. For nearly two years they'd been more like the latter. Any man would be lucky to have her, but the one who'd won her heart had died almost two years ago while bravely serving his country in Afghanistan. Now his two favorite girls were alone.

"You're here earlier than expected. Want a beer?"

"Love one." When Danielle wiggled to get down, Brady

set her on the wooden floor in the big, open great room. "I'm here early because I missed you guys."

Maggie walked around a kitchen island big enough to land a helicopter before stopping in front of the refrigerator. Glancing over her shoulder, she said, "What's wrong, Brady?"

"Nothing." No way he was that easy to read. "Why do you think something's wrong?"

"You look funny." Maggie set his beer on a coaster on the coffee table. "Everything okay at work?"

"Fine." If you didn't factor in him kissing Olivia.

He sat down on the earth-tone woven area rug that covered the middle of the room to play with his niece. Danielle pulled over a wicker toy basket filled with dolls, stuffed animals and fat play figures that fit in her tiny hands. Chattering to herself in a language only she knew, she started unloading her toys one at a time into his lap.

"How are you?" he asked his sister.

"Good. I'm thinking of expanding the ice-cream parlor into the available business space next door. Make it a sandwich shop. With homemade soup. Quiche. Salads made with organic greens. Free-range chicken and grass-fed beef."

Brady held still while his niece crawled onto his thigh and threw a teddy bear out of her way to make room. When she was settled, he braced a hand on her back for stability.

"Are you going to have hamburgers?"

"Hadn't considered it." Maggie sat on the dark-colored sofa and thought for a moment. "Maybe veggie and turkey."

"You don't want it too girly. You want your marketing window open wide. Don't turn off the guys with too much chick food."

"Good point." She smiled fondly at her daughter, who'd pulled a pink feather boa from the bottom of the toy basket and was doing her best to wrap it around Brady's neck. "Speaking of girly…"

"Don't you dare take a picture. No way this leaves your house," he warned.

"Serves you right for buying it."

"I couldn't come home from that San Francisco trip empty-handed."

"Danielle wouldn't know the difference."

"She's smarter than you think. She would know Uncle Brady went away and didn't bring her something." He smiled at the solemn concentration on the little girl's face. "Besides, I'm all about retail bribery to secure her affections."

Maggie beamed at him. "You would be a terrific father, Brady."

"Why? Because I spoil your child?"

"No. Although that's important, too." Her expression turned tender. "Just spending a lot of time with her like you do means so much. Every little girl needs a positive male role model in her life so she knows what to look for when she grows up." Her eyes took on the familiar sadness. "You should have a bunch of kids to fill up that obscenely big house of yours."

"Not likely," he said.

"Surely you have women throwing themselves at you. You're okay-looking if one can ignore those ears."

Brady threw a foam-rubber pink ball in her direction. "Funny."

"Seriously, you're rich and handsome. A pretty good personality. And, quite frankly, you're getting to the age where people are beginning to wonder and ask questions."

Folks in Blackwater Lake gossiped about anything and

everything anyway. But Maggie meant something more. "What are you talking about?"

"You're not getting any younger, and inquiring minds want to know if you're gay. Or if there's some dark and twisted reason for you not getting married and having children."

"I don't need to explain. Let's just call it highly unlikely."

"But why?" Maggie persisted.

"It's not complicated." He watched his niece totter over to pick up the ball and then put it in her mouth. "I'm just not a falling-in-love kind of guy."

And that was the primary reason to acknowledge his not-just-business awareness of Olivia Lawson all these years. Hurting her wasn't an option—and that's what would happen if he started something he had no intention of finishing.

Except a little while ago he *had* started something.

"You're wrong," Maggie said.

"About?"

"Being the falling-in-love sort."

"Oh?" He grabbed his niece and lifted her onto his shoulders, where she squealed with delight and slapped the top of his head with her little hands. "Why do you say that?"

"Here's my theory and worth what you paid for it. Feel free to blow me off." She met his gaze. "You won't let anyone close because you're afraid of losing them. Because it hurts when you lose them."

"Don't quit your day job and take up psychoanalysis," he teased, but there was a lot of truth in her words.

As if she hadn't heard the taunt, Maggie continued. "We lost Dad that Christmas you came home from college."

"Yeah." A trauma like that stayed with a guy forever.

Brady and his father hadn't always been close but then his dad changed jobs, allowing him to be home all the time. He'd coached Brady's baseball team and never missed a high school football game whether or not his son was playing.

He would never forget how his father had collapsed and died in his arms. One minute life was normal and happy, the next it changed forever. And the absence of the man he'd grown to love and emulate was a gaping black hole. It did hurt. So sue him.

"Is there a point to bringing this up?" he asked irritably.

"Then Henry was killed in the accident."

His best friend. The two incidents were a painful lesson that someone you love can suddenly be gone. The only way to keep from hurting was not to care.

Brady met his sister's gaze. "Of all people, you should understand. You lost Dad, too. And then Danny. I know how hard that was on you."

"Still is." The words were spoken softly as she stared at her daughter. "She has his dimples and the shape of his face. Losing him was the worst thing I've ever gone through."

"So you understand why it's unlikely there will ever be anyone special for me."

"No, I really don't." She was still looking at her little girl. "At least I had a great love and know what that feels like."

"If it was so great, why don't you do it again?" Brady countered. "Why aren't *you* dating?"

She sighed. "For one thing, it's not easy when you have a child. How many people want to start a relationship with someone who has a kid?"

"I think you'd be surprised. Look at Adam Stone and Jill Beck. He adopted C.J. after they got married."

"Okay." She thought for a minute. "But then there's Cabot Dixon and Tyler."

Cabot was a good friend of Brady's. His wife had walked out right after Tyler was born and he remained happily single. "Maybe he's not the falling-in-love sort, either."

Maggie made an unladylike snorting noise. "We can trade examples all night, but that won't change what's going on with you."

"And that is?"

"Your only excuse for refusing to open yourself up to love is that you're chicken."

"What is this? Pick-on-Brady day?"

"Did someone else tarnish your image?"

"No way I'm passing this one on. You know how rumors spread here in Blackwater Lake."

"There's a rumor I haven't heard? Don't hold out on me, Brady."

"There's not a chance in hell I'm telling you."

"Language," she said, pointing at her daughter, who was completely oblivious.

"Sorry." And wild horses couldn't drag this particular information out of him.

It was the second time in the last few hours that a woman had dumped on his reputation. He'd shown Olivia his particular kissing skills, although it had backfired big time. But there was nothing he could do or say to convince his sister that in this instance not starting something was for the best.

"So, other than having a child, why are you unwilling to dip your toe in the dating pool?" he challenged.

"It's complicated." She stood. "I'm going to fix dinner now."

"About darn time." He watched her walk into the kitchen. "Please tell me veggie burgers are not on tonight's menu."

"It would serve you right if I served you that and quiche for dessert." She turned and grinned. "But, no. I have a roast in the Crock-Pot."

"Sounds good."

It was the best offer he'd had all day.

Maggie wouldn't talk about it, but she understood the tricky situations dating created. It was like touching a hot stove: after the first time you knew it hurt and avoided another go-round. Things inevitably got complicated when he refused to take a relationship to the next level. Kissing Olivia had taken him somewhere and it was a level he'd never been before.

Now *that* was complicated.

Chapter Five

Olivia had heard somewhere that there were times when retreat was the better part of valor, and at work the day after Brady had kissed her was one of those times. It was almost noon and she'd spent the entire morning avoiding her boss.

She'd known Brady was going to make it hard on her during these last two weeks. As much as she'd wished to be wrong, she hadn't been—but she couldn't really blame him for the kiss. The part about him having a reputation as a bad kisser was fabricated. When had she gotten so good at making stuff up? And why would she do something like that? She knew him well enough to know he'd take it as a challenge. Had she deliberately baited him into kissing her?

It was pathetic and she didn't want to believe that of herself, because she was an honest person and didn't lie. Yet these days she was mostly lying to everyone *but* herself.

Normally when she needed Brady's signature on something, she hopped up and walked into his office. She looked for reasons to see him. Today she was stacking up the paperwork to put on his desk just before she left for the day.

But it would appear that he was avoiding her, too, since he'd been barricaded on the other side of that door since she'd arrived at work today. At least they seemed to be on the same page with that, if not about her quitting her job.

Right now she was going through the calendar, making a list of meetings for the last week of her employment, and it would require her to brief him. By definition that meant she would actually have to see and speak to him— like it or not.

"Uh-oh." Olivia looked at the notation on her schedule. "Darn it. I forgot all about this."

She thought about ignoring it and letting the chips fall where they may, but just couldn't.

Blowing out a long breath, she stood and walked to his office door, then knocked. Loud.

"Come in."

She did and braced for the power of his stare, the one that always went through her like shock waves and made her knees weak. But he didn't look away from his computer screen. So, this morning she'd wasted a lot of energy ignoring him when he was back to treating her like the filing cabinet.

"What is it, Liv? I'm pretty busy."

Oh, really. Did he think she'd been sitting around with an emery board shaping her nails? That wasn't fair. It was about her ego. The kiss had made her feel something, but it hadn't been enough to move him. For him the moment had been about proving something. Good to know. Moving on...

"We have a problem, Brady."

He looked up. "What?"

"Actually, it's your problem, because I'll be gone."

"Okay. Care to enlighten me?"

"Three words. Employee-appreciation weekend."

Now she had his full attention. It was obvious, because he stiffened and swiveled his chair around to look at her. When her gaze went immediately to his mouth, Olivia wished she'd sent this message in an email. The shock waves made her want to step back, so she deliberately moved closer to his desk. She'd show him she didn't feel anything, either. Wow, her morals were going downhill fast. Now even her body language was deceitful.

"What about it?" he asked.

"Six weeks from now, most of your employees will be arriving in Blackwater Lake expecting some show of your appreciation."

"You're kidding, right?"

Yeah, because she needed to make stuff up in order to give herself more work to do. She stood just on the other side of his desk and glared down at him.

"This was your idea five years ago and you dumped it all in my lap. Getting out the memo about transportation reservations and reimbursement. Arranging car service from the airport almost a hundred miles away. Reservations at Blackwater Lake Lodge for everyone. Activities. Awards dinner. Bonuses. Some of it is already done, but not all of it. Just a reminder, I'm here one more week. Last-minute details need to be handled the week before the event. I just thought you should know." Because she couldn't stop looking at his mouth, Olivia noticed when his lips compressed with annoyance. "And now you do."

"Sometimes I wish you weren't quite so efficient."

"And I think you're going to have to cancel it this year."

She folded her arms over her chest and forced her gaze to his forehead, but that wasn't safe either. He was too handsome for his own good, so she looked at the jade monkey on the bookcase just over his shoulder.

"Canceling isn't an option. This event promotes loyalty in the workplace and pays dividends that can't be measured in dollars and cents."

"Like I said, you've got a problem."

"You've always handled it," he said.

"Until now," she amended. "I'm leaving."

When he stood and walked around the desk, Olivia turned her back and headed out of his office. As long as his desk was between them everything was fine, but as soon as she could feel the warmth of his body, her body heated up and shorted out brain function. That reason was as good as any to explain why a normally trustworthy and sincere woman such as herself would goad her too-handsome-for-his-own-good boss into kissing her.

"Liv, wait up."

"I did what I came to do." She sat down at her desk, trying to ignore the fact that he was right behind her. "You've been reminded."

"There's no way I can get everything arranged in time without your help."

"Agreed. You need an assistant." A keeper would be more accurate, but that wasn't her responsibility anymore. She spun her chair around and looked at him. "If you'd taken the interview process seriously and hired someone, I could have trained her. Or him. At least gotten them up to speed on what needs to be done. But you behaved like a petulant little boy who didn't get his way and now there's nothing I can do."

Brady rested his hands on his hips and stared down. His thinking posture, she'd always told him. Usually he came up with a brilliant solution to whatever needed trouble-shooting, but this time she didn't see any way out except to scrub the event. And disappoint a lot of eager, loyal members of his staff.

Then he looked at her and a familiar gleam slid into his green eyes. "I have an idea."

She'd heard that before, but bravely met his gaze. "I'm not going to like it, am I?"

"I can't speak for you, but I don't think Leonard will be too happy." He held up a hand when she opened her mouth. "Just hear me out, Liv."

It was the least she could do before saying no to whatever he had in mind. "I'm listening."

"You haven't put out word yet in the company that you're leaving, right?"

She had not. "That was my next step in order to find someone to fill my job. I know that sometimes you like to hire from the outside to bring new ideas in, but you were wildly uncooperative with every candidate. Now I think promoting from within is the way to go."

"Okay. I get it. My bad." But Brady looked completely unrepentant. "So what would you think about keeping your resignation under wraps for just a little longer?" Again he held up his hand to stop her when she opened her mouth. "Before you lecture me again, it's good business practice to play it that way. Neither the stock market nor the competition need to know that there's any potential shake-up in the works. Especially when it involves someone who works so closely with me."

He had a point. "I see."

"So what do you think about waiting until the awards dinner to announce you're leaving the company?"

"But that means I'd be staying until then."

"I know." He slid his fingertips into the pockets of his jeans.

"I think that would be like waiting to tell the kids about the divorce until after the trip to an amusement park."

"And that's bad—why?"

"It's just putting off the inevitable and feels like a manipulation," she argued.

Brady sighed. "Look, you're right about me. Everything you said about the interviews. I admit it. That wasn't my finest hour."

"You can say that again."

"Don't push it."

"Too much?" she asked sweetly.

"Just a little." The warning lost power when he smiled that appealing smile. "I'll make you a deal."

This was what she dreaded. The moment when he pulled out his charm and set it for stun. Resistance was futile, or at least it would be if she didn't have Leonard to fall back on.

"Leonard is impatient for me to join him. And I can't wait to be with him all the time," she added. "Besides, I don't trust you, Brady."

"Understandable." His eyes glittered when he looked at her mouth. "But it would just be until employee weekend is over."

"And what do I get out of it?"

"You have my word that I'll stop behaving like a spoiled child and hire your replacement—if you'll stay until the event is over."

"Wow." Her eyes narrowed on him. "This is a very different side of you."

"How do you mean?"

"I had no idea you'd become so self-aware and mature about my leaving. Maybe desperation does that."

"Busted. You left me no choice. So, what do you say?" he persisted.

"I'm supposed to start a new job and I was planning to take some time off. A vacation before I pack up and move."

"You could still do that. And I'll hire packers and whoever else you need to make the process as quick and painless as possible."

Darn it all, she was weakening. "But my new job…"

"Surely you can postpone your start date? It's just a few weeks," he coaxed.

"I don't know. It's a really good opportunity and I don't want to jeopardize it."

"Your new boss obviously knows you bring a lot of invaluable skills to the table, since he stole you from me."

"That and he's a friend from college."

"Good. So no problem there." He nodded with satisfaction. "And Leonard…you're worth waiting for. If he doesn't realize that, then he's an idiot."

When Brady moved a little closer, she rolled her chair back and bumped up against the desk. It felt a lot like being a defenseless bug caught in the spider's web.

"I'm not worried about Leonard."

"Okay, then. Problem solved. There's no reason you can't extend your resignation deadline past the employee appreciation event, and I promise to choose someone to take over your job." His expression challenged her to say no. "Deal?"

"Okay." But her heart wasn't in it. Or maybe it *was*— just a little too much.

Brady was finally at a place of tolerance about her quitting, so why wasn't she feeling more relieved? That's when another saying went through her mind. *Be careful what you wish for.* She'd wanted acceptance and now she had it, but the feeling was oddly empty.

"Do you have plans this weekend? With Leonard?" He was trying to look as if he cared, but failed miserably.

"No." They did this every Friday night, talked about what was happening on their days off. "What are you doing?"

"Meeting Cabot Dixon at Bar None."

At least it wasn't a woman. She always faked a supportive look when he told her about his dates and right now she was at her limit of lies. "I'm having dinner with my family."

"That should be fun."

Yes, it should. Unless you had to explain a fake boyfriend and your real reason for moving away from Blackwater Lake.

In Brady's opinion, the best burger in town was served at the Grizzly Bear Diner, but if you wanted a beer on the side Bar None was the place. It was located on the corner of Spruce and Pine Streets, one block west of Main, behind the Grizzly Bear, Potter's Ice-cream parlor and Tanya's Treasures gift shop.

Brady sat in a booth with his friend, rancher Cabot Dixon. The interior of the place was dark, with mahogany walls and a square bar in the middle of the large room. Booths ringed the perimeter with tables scattered in the remaining space. The floor was covered with peanut shells, which would drive a neat freak crazy, but Brady liked it.

Right now he was in the mood to like everything. Olivia had agreed to work for him a little longer. Some would call him a procrastinator, but he figured himself more of a doer. He'd done what was necessary to keep her here through the employee bash. She seemed adamant about leaving, so this reprieve wouldn't change the outcome. He just couldn't deny that he was relieved at not having to say goodbye for a little bit longer.

He cracked open a peanut and dropped the shells on the floor just because he could. "How you been, Cabot?"

"Can't complain. You?"

"Good. Have you heard Tiffani Guthrie might be coming back to town?"

"Do I know her?"

"Probably not, if you have to ask." He stared, assessing his friend. The man had dark hair and eyes that were nearly black. Women definitely took note of the tall rancher.

Cabot caught the look and frowned. "What?"

"My mother said I should alert you about her."

"Why would I need a warning about your mother?"

"No. Tiffani. Mom said you're a good-looking, rich man and I should give you a heads-up that she's looking for a rescue from the bad situation she landed in." He took the man's measure again. "And I guess Mom is right. You're not a bad-looking guy."

The other man held up his hands. "Don't get the wrong idea about why I asked you here."

"You mean we're not having a bromance?"

"I don't know what that is," Cabot said. "But I don't like the sound of it."

"It's a combination of *brother* and *romance*. Olivia told me about it." His assistant wasn't just the smartest and most organized he'd ever had, she kept him up-to-date socially and with current cultural references. He was going to miss that. "Don't get your spurs bent out of shape. It just means two guys who are good friends."

"Wouldn't it be easier to say that?" Then Cabot grinned. "You had me worried for a minute. So, Tiffani?"

"Yeah. I met her when we were seniors in high school and she dumped me my last year in college. Apparently she married a guy who worked on oil rigs. But according to my mother, things haven't gone so well in the double-wide trailer with her husband in North Armpit Falls, Texas. And she's on her way back to Blackwater Lake to rekindle things with me because now I'm not a penniless college dropout."

"So, is it a good thing?" Cab took a drink of his beer. "Her coming back, I mean."

"It's not good or bad. It's…" Brady shrugged, trying to come up with the right word. "Nothing."

"Then you have nothing to worry about."

"My mother thinks *you* might." Brady pointed the long neck of his beer bottle in his friend's direction. "You've got more than a few bucks."

"I do okay."

In fact, Cabot Dixon was very well off. There was money in land, cattle, horses and mineral rights.

"A woman could do worse than you," he pointed out.

"Not looking for one."

"Still…" Brady knew the man's experience with marriage had been bad. "It's been a long time."

"Not long enough." Cabot took a peanut from the basket and cracked it with more force than necessary. "And *still* not interested."

"Okay, then. My work here is done. You've been warned." Brady wished someone had warned him about kissing Olivia. He was having a devil of a time keeping his mouth away from hers. Looking at her lips and not going there again was testing his willpower and he was trying the "out of sight, out of mind" philosophy. So far it wasn't working very well, because he'd hunkered down in his office and still couldn't stop thinking about kissing her again.

Fortunately, the waitress picked that moment to stop at the end of the booth. She was in her late twenties with blond hair and blue eyes, dressed in worn jeans and a snap-front shirt. An apron with pockets was tied around her trim waist and she pulled an order pad from it. Her name tag read Ronnie.

"So, have you made up your minds or do you need more time?" she asked.

"Burger," Cab said. "The works."

"Me, too."

"Coming right up." She scooped their menus from the end of the table. "Do you need another beer?"

They both declined and she disappeared.

"So, Cab, what can I do for you? You said you wanted to ask my advice about computers."

His friend nodded as he cracked another shell and popped the nut in his mouth. "I'm looking to replace the one I've got. It's old and limping along. If you asked me about running a ranch, I could bend your ear for hours, but computers are a mystery to me. Before making a move, I wanted some expert input. Figured it's in your wheelhouse, what with running a technology company."

Brady had done pretty well in the field. Designing software had earned him the capital to start his own company and he'd never looked back. "Tell me what your needs are."

"I keep ranch records on it. Not just financial. I've got spreadsheets on the horses and cattle, too."

"What else?"

"I want to do a new website. Professional. For the summer camp. A virtual tour of the facilities and everything we have to offer. I'm thinking about expanding."

"The camp is really important to you." It wasn't a question.

Cab nodded. "As my son gets older, I can see the benefits of experiencing the outdoors. Can't imagine raising him anywhere else. But a lot of kids don't get that except once a year."

"I can set up a system for you," Brady said. "And I'll hook you up with a guy who's a website designer. Really gifted, creatively and technologically."

"Is he here in town?"

Brady shook his head. "He works remotely. Manages that division of O'Keefe Technology. We met in college. His name is Ian Bradshaw."

"That would be great. I was hoping you'd have a name. Wasn't looking forward to researching that."

"Now that I think about it," Brady said, "he's coming to Blackwater Lake for the annual employee weekend. I'll have him come in a few days early and send him your way."

"Great." His friend took a sip of beer. "A new web design would help me get the word out without too much of a time investment for me."

"So, you're busy."

"Between ranching and raising my son?" Cabot laughed. "There aren't enough hours in the day to get everything done that needs doing."

"How old is Tyler now?"

"Eight." The man smiled and all the world-weariness slipped away. There was a mixture of love and tenderness in his voice. Clearly he was a proud father.

Brady remembered what his sister had said when he played with his niece. That he would be a good father and it was a shame he wasn't moving in that direction.

He'd thought about it a lot, and watching Maggie with

her daughter had released a feeling of yearning that he'd never experienced before. It was different. Strange. Impossible.

"You're a single dad, Cabot. How is that working out for you?"

"Being a father is the hardest and most rewarding job I've ever done." He toyed with his bottle of beer and tenderness gave way to tension on his face. "You know he was only a couple weeks old when his mother walked out."

"That must have been hard."

"There are no words to describe how hard." Now anger swirled in his eyes. "I'd never even changed a diaper before. Yeah, I raised animals on the ranch, but that's a whole lot different from being responsible for a baby. You don't have to get up to feed a cow or horse every two or three hours. And there are no sleepless nights walking the floor with a fussy and teething puppy or calf." He shrugged. "It's not for wimps."

"And you did it all alone."

"I had Martha Spooner to watch him during the day. She mostly does housekeeping work now, but when Ty was little she'd come by because a lot of ranch work isn't baby friendly. But nights it was Ty and me."

"He's a great kid. You're doing a terrific job with him."

"Thanks."

Ronnie the waitress brought their burgers and fries. "Anything else I can get you? Ketchup? Steak sauce? Another beer?"

"Nothing for me."

"Me either," Cab said.

They ate in silence for a few moments, then Brady grabbed some napkins from the table dispenser and wiped his mouth. "Where is Ty tonight?"

"Sleepover at C.J.'s house."

Brady knew he meant Jill Beck Stone's little boy who'd been adopted by Dr. Adam Stone, the man who relocated to Blackwater Lake and rented the apartment upstairs from her. Now they had a baby and were building a sprawling house in the same luxury home development where his was located. There was another kid who'd spent some time in a single parent home, but C.J. and his mom got lucky. He couldn't help thinking about Maggie.

He and his sister had lost their own dad far too soon, but at least not in his formative years. Brady tried to be there for his niece as much as possible but would that be enough?

He looked at Cabot. "I'm concerned about my niece not growing up with two parents."

"Yeah." Cabot finished the last of his hamburger then squirted ketchup on the plate for the fries. "It had to be tough on Maggie losing her husband."

"I had my folks when I was a kid, but you're dealing with it on your own. Any words of wisdom?"

"You were lucky." There was more his friend didn't say, but his eyes narrowed with memories. "The way I see it, life is about playing the hand you're dealt. It's about building character. I figure I've got plenty of it to spare. Do I wish I could give Ty a childhood that's normal? Yeah. Of course. But I had no say. That horse left the barn when my wife walked away from her infant son."

In a nutshell, that was why Cabot Dixon wasn't looking for or interested in a woman. Brady felt the same way—but for a different reason. Caring about someone left you open and vulnerable to a pain that could happen anytime, anyplace, for any reason. So he didn't let himself care.

Take Olivia, for instance. She was leaving and he expected that after she was gone nothing would feel normal. Then again, his normal had changed when he'd kissed her.

Before that kiss, her quitting would have been about losing an exceptional employee. Now he had to find a way to go back to the place where losing her couldn't touch him deep down inside.

Chapter Six

Olivia pulled her compact car to a stop in front of her parents' home, a two-story house three doors down from Maureen O'Keefe's. This was where she'd grown up, three doors down from where Brady had lived. She'd nursed her crush on him in the upstairs dormer bedroom, a stone's throw away from where he'd spent the nights of his youth.

The home where Olivia had grown up was a white clapboard, four-bedroom place with hunter-green trim, shutters and front door. There was a wrought-iron glider on the covered porch where her parents sat in the evening when the weather was nice. More often than not, Brady's mom would wander over and sit on one of the cushioned chairs that were there for neighbors who dropped by.

She turned off the engine and drew in a deep breath against the stunning pain squeezing her heart. It suddenly hit her that when she moved away to California all of this, everything familiar, would be far away. Her whole life would change.

But wasn't that what she'd wanted?

Before Brady kissed her, the answer to that question was a resounding yes. Now? The only thing she knew for sure was a deep and persistent confusion. And that she wasn't looking forward to this family dinner as much as usual, not only because of the conversation they would have but because family dinners would be few and far between.

Her younger sister's car was parked at the curb in front of her. Prudence had left room for her and that thought had the backs of her eyes stinging with tears.

"Olivia Lawson, stop it right now," she said to herself.

In order to sell her move as a happy thing to her family, it would be helpful to actually look happy.

She exited the car and dragged in a breath when the bitter cold hit her. Snow from a recent storm still lingered on the ground where shadows from the trees and house sheltered it. She moved up the sidewalk and knocked once on the door before letting herself inside. "Hello? Anyone home?"

"In the kitchen." That was her mother's voice from the room where she could usually be found, except on weekdays, when she taught fourth grade at Blackwater Lake Elementary. "We've been waiting for you."

Tears welled, again because someday very soon no one would be waiting for her.

Olivia looked around the living room she'd spent so much of the last twenty-seven years in—as an infant, toddler, child, young adult, college student. Pictures on the oak mantel above the fireplace told her story without words. She never thought she would leave the town where she'd been born. How would the pictures change?

Footsteps sounded on the light-colored wood floor just before her mother walked into the room. "Hey, sweetie."

"Hi, Mom." She hugged her mother more tightly than usual. "How are you?"

"Doing great." Ann Lawson was the same height as her daughter, a blue-eyed blonde with a pixie cut. After a breast cancer diagnosis five years ago, she'd had chemo and lost her hair. When it grew back, she'd decided to keep it short and easy. She pulled back and frowned. "How are you?"

"Fine."

Her mother didn't look convinced, but said nothing more. "Your father and sister are anxious to see you. We all want to hear about your exciting news."

Arm in arm they walked down the hall, past the formal dining room with its cherrywood table and matching china cabinet. Ahead was the kitchen/great room that was the command-and-control center of the home. Through the years this was where they gathered and it was a comfort that some things didn't change.

A leather corner group sat in front of a flat-screen TV mounted on the wall above a fireplace with a roaring fire going. Her father was director of the local power company and would be busy when the next snowstorm hit, but right now he was relaxing on the sofa, watching a football game with Prudence.

They both looked up and smiled when she entered the room.

"Hi, Livvie." Ken Lawson was a still-handsome fifty-two-year-old man with silver streaking his dark hair and neatly trimmed mustache.

"Good to see you, Dad."

"Hey, sis." Prudence stood and walked over to hug her.

She was quite simply gorgeous and had inherited their father's dark hair and gray eyes.

"Hi, Pru." Olivia gave her an extra squeeze, then pulled back and pasted a smile on her face. "What's going on?"

Her dad joined them by the kitchen island and slung his arm across her shoulders, pulling her close. "You're the one with the news. Tell your old man what you're up to."

She rested her cheek against his solid shoulder for a moment, then met his gaze. "A friend of mine from college is starting a technology company and asked if I'd be interested in working with him."

"So you get in on the ground floor?"

"That's right, Dad. The only catch is that the job is in California."

"That makes commuting out of the question," he said.

How like her father to defuse a situation with humor. Unfortunately she didn't feel much like smiling. "But when he mentioned that my title would be vice president, it got my attention."

"I guess so." Her father looked down and there was pride in his expression. "A good manager can spot talent when he sees it."

"Right now it doesn't mean much, but…" She shrugged. "And you're prejudiced."

"Nope. I'm not just saying that because you're my little girl."

Pru made a scoffing sound. "You're such a liar, Dad."

Maybe that's where she'd gotten the gene for being an exemplary fibber, Olivia thought. "I'm just glad Colin has faith in me. That's my friend—Colin Buchanan."

"I've met him," her sister said. "He's cute. Smart, too. Did he get married?"

"No." Olivia held up a finger when her sister showed signs of asking more. "And I don't know anything else."

"Actually…" Pru put on her injured expression. "I was going to ask about your mysterious boyfriend who doesn't live here."

He didn't live anywhere besides her imagination, Olivia thought. But obviously her mother had passed on what she'd been told on the phone. Olivia hated lying in general, but particularly disliked deceiving the people she loved most in the world. The problem was that if she came clean about Leonard, her mother would tell Maureen because the women were best friends. As they always said, the bond had been forged through the fire of raising children and nothing could break it. As soon as the cat was out of the bag, Mrs. O'Keefe would pass the news on to Brady.

She couldn't tell the truth yet, but downplaying Leonard would set the stage for dumping him as soon as she left her job.

"I understand his name is Leonard." Her mother's question was nonchalant, which meant she was working hard at keeping her voice neutral.

"Really, Liv. Leonard?" Pru wrinkled her cute little nose. "Does he at least have a cool middle name you could use? Like Jack, Carson or Brad?"

"No. It's Sebastian." And she didn't have a clue where that came from any more than she did about the lie that started her down this cursed path. Might as well go for broke. "Leonard Sebastian Honeycut."

The three of them stared at her for several moments. It wasn't often her family was speechless and she was kind of glad about it now. The fewer questions they asked, the less she had to lie.

"Where did you meet him?" Ann pulled plates out of the cupboard and set them on the granite-topped island.

"I had a trip to San Francisco." That was no lie. "And I

made a detour to see Colin in Southern California." Also true. They could connect the dots. "It all worked out."

"I can't wait to meet him," Prudence said. "What does he look like?"

Oh, dear Lord. "I don't know," she said. "Average."

"Sense of humor?" her mother wanted to know.

"Just like mine."

"That's very important." She looked fondly at her husband. "That's what gets you through the years."

Olivia agreed. Brady had a wonderful sense of humor.

"I just want you to know how much I admire what you're doing." Her sister nodded with conviction. "You love Leonard and the two of you are going all in and making a commitment to each other. I respect that so much. And you've got a great new job, too!"

Although Olivia wanted to tell Pru not to use her as a role model, there was really nothing she could say that wouldn't raise a lot of questions. And that would lead to more untruths. She'd had enough of that to last a lifetime.

"Thanks, Pru," she finally said.

Her mother assembled forks, knives and napkins. "Ken, Pru, why don't you set the table in the dining room? Oh, and find those beautiful crystal wineglasses in the china cabinet. We need to toast the good news. The lasagna is almost ready. Livvie can help me with salad and garlic bread."

"Okay, honey." Her husband saluted, his eyes twinkling. "Pru and I won't let you down."

"Smart aleck."

"It's a dirty job, but someone has to do it."

Olivia was glad to have something to keep her busy. She got spring greens and fresh vegetables from the refrigerator, then the wooden salad bowl to put it all in. "It smells good in here, Mom."

"I'm glad." Using mitts, Ann pulled the baking dish out of the oven. "So, when did you plan to tell us you were in love, had a new job and were leaving town?"

The sudden question startled her and she turned to look at her mother. In the blue eyes so like her own, she saw the same pain she'd experienced a little while ago when pulling up out front. Her words had to be as close to the truth as possible.

"This change isn't about Leonard and I'm not moving because of him. That was just what I told Brady to keep him from talking me into staying again. I need to shake up my life, Mom."

"You can't just find another job here in Blackwater Lake?"

"No."

"Because Brady would still be here," her mother said. "You know?"

"Of course. I'm your mother. I know you. I see the way you look at him."

"Remind me not to play poker with you." Olivia sighed. "Excitement has passed me by for the last five years and if I don't do something, another five will go by and nothing will change."

Her mom stared at her as if she could see straight into her heart and soul. Then she nodded. "I understand."

"If not for Leonard, I'll weaken and Brady will talk me into staying." She blew out a breath. "He already convinced me to stay until after the annual employee weekend."

"I see."

"After that, I'm taking a vacation. When I start work with Colin, it will probably be brutal hours and not much time off. I haven't had a break in a long time."

"That sounds like a good plan, sweetie."

"Thanks for understanding, Mom." She smiled. "I'll be back for visits all the time and you guys can come see me. The Golden State. You and Dad will love it. But I have to go. If I don't, I'll never find a life."

And it hurt too much not to have one.

It was almost quitting time on Monday and Olivia was ready to be finished for the day. On top of trying to clean up work so as not to overwhelm her replacement, details for employee-appreciation weekend had to be handled. In addition to all that, Brady had asked her to contact Ian Bradshaw and make sure he could come in a few days early to consult with Cabot Dixon on a summer-camp website. That was taken care of.

Lately she was doing more with less—sleep, that was. Telling her family about relocating had been stressful and emotional. She didn't even want to think about how awful it would be when she finally moved, but move she must to get out of her personally unfulfilling rut. A clean break was the only way.

She heard the beep, the deactivated security system's warning that someone had opened the front door. Moments later her sister, Prudence, appeared in her office.

"Hi, Liv." She looked upset.

Olivia stood up behind her desk. "Are you okay?"

"I was wondering if you wanted to go to Bar None and get a drink after work."

"Sounds good. I could use one. Been a busy day."

"I can use one, too," Pru said, her mouth trembling. "Because my day was just awful."

"What happened?" She was around the desk in a heart-beat. "Tell me—"

The door to Brady's office opened. "Prudence Lawson, as I live and breathe." He must have heard the beep and surfaced, checking out who was there. "To what do we owe the honor of a visit from Blackwater Lake High School's most popular chemistry teacher?"

Big gray eyes welled with tears. When they rolled down Pru's cheeks, she buried her face in her hands. In a heartbeat Olivia was holding her.

Brady was beside them. "What's wrong?"

A horrible thought occurred to Olivia. "Is it Mom? Dad—"

"No." Pru looked up. "Gosh, no. I'm sorry. Compared to that, what happened is so unimportant, but—" Tears glistened in her eyes again. "Greg dumped me."

"Oh, sweetie—" Olivia urged her sister into one of the club chairs in front of her desk. She sat in the other one.

"Isn't he the high-school football coach?" Brady asked.

Her sister nodded. "And he teaches math."

"I thought you two were getting serious. Last night at Mom and Dad's you told me that he was close to proposing."

"I was wr-wrong."

"What happened?" Olivia asked.

"After we talked last night I started thinking."

"Uh-oh." Brady settled a hip on the corner of her desk. "Thinking is never a good idea."

That got a small smile. "We've been going out almost a year. Liv, I was just so impressed with the way you and Leonard are in sync and going forward with your relationship."

Olivia wanted to cry now. She was the last person her sister should listen to or take advice from. "Oh, sweetie, you and I are different people."

"And Greg is no Leonard, that's for sure," Pru said angrily. "When the going got tough, he got going. I brought up the subject of commitment and he said he wasn't ready.

That we weren't on the same page and it would be for the best if we stopped seeing each other."

"Toad." Olivia was so angry. She wanted to hurt the guy who'd hurt the baby sister she loved so much. "I'd like to give him an earful."

"Want me to beat him up for you?" Brady asked.

"Would you?" Pru asked hopefully.

"Just say the word. But before I defend your honor, there are a couple of things you should consider. These are in no particular order, but it's from the male point of view. That might be helpful."

"Please." Her sister made a hand gesture that urged him to go on.

Olivia was intensely curious about what he would say. He seemed so clueless about feelings and getting relationship advice from a guy who didn't commit could be problematic.

"Think about this." Brady folded his arms over his chest. "You're better off that he broke up with you."

"How can you say that?" Olivia cried. "She loves him."

"And that's unfortunate. At the risk of inciting the wrath of both Lawson sisters, Greg is right. You want commitment, he obviously doesn't. As he said, not the same page. So, to continue as you are would be a waste of time. Move on. Find someone who's looking for and ready to commit to a wonderful, beautiful, smart woman like you."

"Just like that?" Olivia asked. "Go find someone else?"

He looked at her calmly, as if she were a hysterical child. "I'm not saying it's easy, but isn't it worse to invest time in a relationship that is clearly going nowhere?"

"When you put it that way…" Pru said reluctantly.

"But he hurt her." This was her sister and Olivia wanted toad guy punished, preferably with pain involved.

"Believe it or not, most men don't like calling it quits with a woman, deliberately hurting them. But if you don't want the same things, ultimately it won't work out. The sooner you break it off, the sooner you can get over him and move forward. So, look at it this way, Pru."

"I'm listening."

"He actually did you a favor."

His calm, rational tone finally got through and Olivia thought about his words. It was exactly what she was doing, although Brady certainly hadn't done *her* any favors. He'd kissed her, then nothing since. That was proof that it meant nothing to him and moving on was the right thing for her.

"I didn't think about it like that." Prudence sniffled and he handed her a tissue from the box on Olivia's desk.

"Me, either," Olivia admitted. "Same thing applies to a woman dumping a man. If they aren't on the same page, she's doing him a favor in the long run."

"Absolutely."

Who knew that a guy who understood computers as though they were his best friends could give such great relationship advice? He'd actually coaxed a smile from heartbroken Pru. He was showing some very definite symptoms of being wonderful. This man would understand if she explained that she was feeling stifled and needed to go out into the world, stopping short of confessing her crush, of course. But the rest he would get.

Olivia felt like pond scum for fibbing about a boyfriend. She'd underestimated Brady and would come clean as soon as her sister left.

But Pru didn't seem inclined to leave the love guru's office. "I feel so much better, Brady. When did you get so smart?"

He shrugged. "It's not about IQ. What I said is just logical."

"That's where men and women are different," Olivia said. "When emotion is involved, logic goes out the window. We're wired differently."

"And that's a good thing. It's about balance," he said sagely.

Prudence crushed the tissue in her palm and smiled at him as if he'd hung the moon. "You, sir, are pretty amazing. How is it that no woman has snapped you up?"

He laughed. "I appreciate the kind words, but it's not miraculous insight. Like I said, just common sense."

"Yet sensitive," Pru persisted.

Olivia looked from her sister to her boss. "I've never heard anyone accuse you of being sensitive before."

"I can be." There was a twinkle in his eyes as he looked at her. "You're just too stressed out about leaving me for Leonard and finding your replacement to see it."

"Oh, please."

"He could be right, Liv. Because I thought it was going to take a bottle of wine to make me feel better and Brady took care of it with a conversation. Saving me a hangover, by the way. That's seriously sensitive." She tapped her lip as she studied him. "And you're still single."

"I am."

"What's wrong with the women of Blackwater Lake? Surely they're interested."

"I can't complain."

Olivia wanted to raise her hand and admit to being one of the interested, but held back. As it turned out, she was glad about that.

"So again I ask, why is it that you have avoided taking any relationship to the next level?" Pru asked.

"That's easy to answer," he said.

Pru glanced at her, then met his gaze. "So tell us."

"I'm not a marrying kind of guy." He shrugged, as if that said it all.

"No woman has tempted you to take the plunge?" her sister asked.

"It never goes that far. Like I said, a waste of time for everyone involved."

They continued to talk, but Olivia felt a buzzing in her head and couldn't concentrate on what was said. She was stunned at his revelation, but she should have realized it. After all these years, and who knew how many women, he'd never had a serious connection.

She would have known. Blackwater Lake was a small town and there was no way to keep that kind of thing a secret. But there was something shocking about hearing him confess the truth out loud. It was imperative for her to get away from this job while she still could.

As if the kiss wasn't warning enough, his declaration that he would never get married convinced her she was leaving in the nick of time. Her decision to make up a lover in order to pull it off wasn't *morally* right, but made perfect sense when one was into self-preservation. The fact that Brady's words bothered her so much convinced her not to feel too guilty about her lies.

She wanted what her parents had. And to accomplish that, she had to do anything and everything necessary to leave Blackwater Lake. No matter what.

So, until she was free and clear, Leonard Sebastian Honeycut was here to stay.

Chapter Seven

It was almost quitting time, and Olivia looked at the watch on her wrist. Yesterday at this time her sister had dropped by and cried over the messy breakup with her boyfriend. Then Brady had given her straight talk, so straight he'd revealed that he wasn't the kind of guy who was looking to get married.

That was confirmation that she'd been right to give her notice and get away from this job, from him. Maybe "right" wasn't exactly the best way to describe her strategy of deceit to follow through with leaving, but there was one bright spot. She looked at her watch again.

"It's been a whole twenty-four hours since I told a lie about Leonard."

Just then the phone rang, startling her. It was like a reminder from God that she still had a pile of deceptions to be accountable for. The penance Brady was putting her through now probably didn't wipe her record clean.

After the third ring she picked up and said, "O'Keefe Technology, Olivia speaking. How can I help you?"

"Hi, Liv. It's Maureen."

"Hey. How are you?"

"Been better," she mumbled. "Is Brady there?"

"I'm sorry, he isn't. He had some errands to run but should be back soon. Is there anything I can do?"

"Yes. You can keep that hussy away from my son."

"What hussy would that be?" she asked his mother.

"Tiffani Guthrie." She spat out the name as if it were a particularly fast-acting poison. "I have visual confirmation that she's back in town."

"You saw her?"

"At the diner," she confirmed. "I didn't talk to her, but Michelle Crawford did and told me that all the rumors are true about why she's back in town."

Great, Olivia thought. Because there wasn't enough to deal with. The hussy couldn't have waited until she was gone before stirring things up. "Do you want him to call you when he gets back?"

"That's not necessary," the other woman said. "Just give him the message. And tell him to watch his back."

"Consider it done, Maureen."

"Thank you, Liv." There was a moment of hesitation before she added, "Why couldn't he be involved with you?"

"I'm sorry?"

"You're such a sweetie. If you two were an item, he'd have cover. Tiffani couldn't get to him. Except there's Leonard…"

If she didn't say anything in response to that, was it still officially a lie? That would break a very short falsehood-free streak. It was nice to know Brady's mother would approve of a relationship between them, but the information was bittersweet. Olivia wished he'd noticed her in that way, but it wasn't to be. She'd thought pain was supposed to go away when you stopped beating your head against the wall. So far that wasn't the case.

"Do you think Brady still cares for Tiffani?"

"He says not, but he did once. I know the breakup hurt him. If there's a God in heaven, she won't be able to do it again," Maureen said.

"I'll do what I can." Olivia decided it would be best not to add that there wasn't actually anything she could do. If Brady was still hung up, he'd take it wherever he wanted. "Don't worry."

"Yeah, that will happen."

She heard the chirp indicating that someone had entered the house. "I know it's hard. But you have to trust Brady."

At that moment he walked into the room and heard his name. He frowned and pointed to the phone in her hand, asking who she was talking to. On a scratch pad she wrote, "Your mom," and gave him a questioning look that asked if he wanted to speak with her. He shook his head and mouthed, "Take a message." She nodded and turned her attention back to the conversation.

"He's a man," Maureen was saying, "and as you probably know since you're practically engaged to Leonard, men don't always use their heads. When it comes to women, especially ones with big—"

"Hair?" Olivia guessed.

Maureen laughed. "I was thinking boobs, but she's been living in Texas, so I guess that's appropriate. Although it would be an affront to Texas women to lump her in with them. Ellie Hart, that lovely girl Alex McKnight is engaged to, comes from the Lone Star state and there's not a mean or manipulative bone in her body."

In other words, Tiffani was both of those things. Olivia

had seen her when Brady dated her, but she didn't really know the woman.

"Don't borrow trouble, Maureen. Brady has a lot of common sense." She turned and saw him standing in the doorway between their offices. He was grinning and giving her a nod of approval for her vote of confidence. Since when did reassuring his mother fall under her job description? His ego needed taking down a peg or two. "Like all men, he can be influenced by a well-endowed woman. Seriously, wouldn't you worry if he weren't?"

He mouthed, "Hey, that's my mom," and she threw him a satisfied smirk.

"A mother worries about everything," the other woman confirmed.

"Hang in there, Maureen. I'm sure everything will be fine."

"From your mouth to God's ear. I wish you weren't leaving him. With you there it was one less thing I worried about."

"How sweet of you to say that." Her voice caught on the emotion produced by the unexpected compliment. "I promise I'll give him the message."

"Thanks, sweetheart. Bye."

The line went dead and Olivia put the phone back in its place, then prepared for a barrage of questions from Brady.

"So, I'm influenced by a woman's physical virtues?"

"Your mom said it first." To his credit, Olivia thought, he kept his gaze on hers. But then, maybe she didn't have any physical virtues to speak of.

"May I ask what this is all about?" He didn't look annoyed, just highly amused.

"She called to give you the four-one-one—"

"Excuse me?"

"Information," she explained. "That hussy—her words,

not mine—Tiffani Guthrie is back in town. She had visual confirmation. Again, her words."

He nodded. "I heard."

"Good news travels fast."

Try as she might, Olivia couldn't tell from his expression what was going through his mind. He wasn't angry or upset, happy or excited. His face was blank, as if wiped clean of emotion.

Did that mean he was over Tiffani? Or, like he'd said yesterday, that he wasn't interested in getting serious? The curiosity was too much for her and she really wanted to know. She was leaving anyway. What could it hurt?

"Can I ask you something?"

"Sure. Anything." He moved around the front of her desk and settled a hip on the corner. "Shoot."

Olivia was momentarily tongue-tied. The spicy scent of his cologne wrapped her in a sensuous cocoon, swirling a spell around her. For just a second she pictured herself in his arms, their lips pressed tightly together, bodies so close it was as if they were one. Her pulse quickened and she couldn't seem to catch her breath.

"Liv? What did you want to ask?" he prompted.

She shook her head to clear it of the erotic image. If she was going to speak, breathing was a vital component. *Here goes,* she thought.

"I was just wondering. Is Tiffani the reason you're not the marrying kind? Did she hurt you that much?"

"It was a bad time for me." For just a second there was a pained expression on his face, then it disappeared. "Senior year in college. There was a lot of stuff going on. Exams coming up. I just—" He dragged his fingers through his hair. "It's hard to explain being a quitter, but I just didn't have the reserves to stay in college. Not then."

"So you were vulnerable?"

He shrugged. "Bottom line is that she didn't have faith in me, so she said we were over."

"That must have hurt a lot."

"It's so long ago I don't even remember how I felt."

"So," she said, "after that you became cynical about women?"

"No. I realized she did me a favor."

It took Olivia a few seconds for her brain to switch gears enough to ask, "What?"

"I'm actually grateful to her for breaking it off."

"Why?"

"It was a lesson that took some time to integrate." He looked thoughtful. "But I finally figured out that she found someone else pretty quickly."

"Meaning?" Olivia wanted to hear him say it.

"She didn't love me. We were a habit and when she walked away I didn't miss her. It never would have worked with us. After awhile it became clear that deep feelings aren't part of my skill set."

"And that's why you're antimarriage?"

"Not for other people, only for me. It requires deep feeling, a level of commitment from both parties or it's doomed to failure. And failure is a bitter pill to swallow. I can tell you that from personal experience." There was disappointment on his face that was clearly self-directed. "I've always regretted not getting my college degree."

"You could have gone back," she pointed out.

"I was committed to building the company, and that didn't allow time for erasing regrets."

"So you're still beating yourself up over it even though you're one of the most brilliant and successful business-men in the country?"

"Even though," he confirmed. "As a life lesson, it earned me at least a master's degree, possibly a PhD. But it's also a valuable warning. Never start something you're not going to finish because it's a regret waiting to happen."

"Okay, then," she said. "You need to reassure your mom that you're not susceptible to female—"

"Assets?" His look was wickedly endearing.

"Exactly."

"I can do that." He grinned, then stood and walked around the desk, standing so close that she could feel the heat from his body. "I'll call her now."

Olivia held her breath until he'd closed his office door, then let it out as she dropped into her desk chair. She wasn't sure how she'd expected him to answer her question—but what he'd said hadn't been it. He came from such a supportive and close-knit family and she knew he loved them very much. He *was* capable of deep emotion. Just not the kind of deep emotion required for a relationship.

That's when she realized what just happened. They said curiosity killed the cat but it had done the same thing to hope.

She wished she'd never asked.

"Don't you think this thing with Olivia's boyfriend is weird?"

Brady had gone to his sister's house following a call to his mother to reassure her that he could handle Tiffani Guthrie if necessary. Now he was stretched out on Maggie's couch, feet on the coffee table after dinner. His niece was asleep and his sister was a good friend of Olivia's and might be able to give him some insight. But when his question went unanswered, he looked over and noted a funny look on her face.

"Well?" he prompted.

"If I were you, I'd be more concerned about Tiffani Guthrie."

He held a half-empty bottle of beer and rested it on his abdomen. "Mom said something similar. What is it with you and her?"

"She—Tiffani, not Mom—is a barracuda. You're a wealthy man now. It's pretty obvious." Maggie sat in the chair beside him with her feet propped on the matching ottoman.

She was wearing fleece cartoon-character pants, fuzzy slippers and a Green Bay Packers sweatshirt. On her it looked good, but that was about her fresh-faced prettiness. Although he could be prejudiced. Then what she'd said sank in.

"It's not obvious to me why I should be concerned about an old girlfriend."

"Come on, Brady." She snorted scornfully. "You weren't good enough for her before."

"Thanks, sis. Way to build up my self-esteem."

"But now you've got a bundle of money and I'm sure you'll be worth her time. Plus—" She held up her index finger. "There's the whole her-marriage-is-over thing, not to mention the life lessons of living in a single-wide in the boonies."

"So you think she came back for me?"

"No. Your money would help to finance a lifestyle to which she'd like to become accustomed." Her brown eyes darkened with fierce protectiveness. "Watch yourself."

"Look, Mags, I appreciate that you're trying to protect me. I'm flattered you think I'm such a catch—"

"I'm sorry. You thought that's what I meant?" She grinned. "Actually, in my humble opinion, you're a toad."

"Lest there be any doubt, in our family there's no danger of developing a swelled head."

"Seriously, Brady, don't get sucked in. She did a number on you once."

"Not really."

It wasn't committing to one person that he shied away from, but pinning hopes, dreams and love on one person who could be snatched away in a heartbeat. Olivia had advised him to assure his mom that he was over the past. Dumping the information on Maggie was almost as good. It would get where it needed to go.

"Look, sis, Tiffani did me a favor when she ended things. It was clear she didn't love me and I realized we'd gotten used to each other. A habit. I didn't miss her when she left, and that's not love."

"Good." She was holding a mug of tea in her hands and took a sip. "But that doesn't mean she won't try again now that you're rich."

"Oh, please." This was getting old. "It's obvious why she came back. The marriage ended and this is her hometown. She has family. It's the logical thing to do."

"Okay. If you say so."

"I'm more concerned about Olivia."

"Why?" Maggie's expression was full of innocence— on steroids.

"I can't believe I'm the only one who sees this." There was something going on and he had a sneaking suspicion that his saintly sister was in on it. He watched her closely. "Olivia is leaving Blackwater Lake for a man no one knows. Doesn't that bother you? It's what Tiffani did, and look what happened to her."

"You have a point," she admitted. "I'm afraid this guy is going to hurt Olivia. Brady, you have to do something to stop it."

"Me?" He sat up straight and put his feet on the floor.

"She's found someone and is willing to move for him. What can I do?"

"Leonard is nothing."

Something in Maggie's tone had warning signals going off in his head. His sister wasn't a very good liar and that had his suspicions multiplying like bunnies. "What's going on, Maggie?"

"I have no idea what you're talking about."

"Yeah, you do. Like I said, this thing with Leonard is weird. Have you met him?"

"No."

"It's like she pulled him out of a hat. He's not from around here or we'd know. She never mentioned him until giving me notice that she was quitting the company. She doesn't see him. I'd know because she'd have to travel for that. He never visits or everyone here in Blackwater Lake would know. There's nothing in her email—"

"You didn't."

"Of course I did."

"You looked at her personal email messages?" Maggie stared at him. "That's an invasion of privacy. Really, Brady, I'm shocked and appalled."

"That's interesting. She took it better than you."

"Olivia knows what you did?"

"Yes," he said cheerfully. "She caught me in the act."

His sister shook her head. "You should be ashamed of yourself."

"I will be. Maybe next week. In the meantime, I need to figure out what's up. The more I think about it, the more convinced I am that something is funny. Not ha-ha, but weird funny."

"I don't think she loves him. Not yet. But she could get hurt."

"I thought so, too," he said, ignoring the part about

Olivia getting hurt. "This thing she's got going on just doesn't seem like it's on the way to love."

"How would you know?" his sister demanded. "You're not a falling-in-love kind of guy. What is that saying? Oh, yeah. Takes one to know one."

"Not really. It's deductive reasoning. How can you make plans to move away from family, friends and a really good job for a man you never see? That's just crazy. Or strange."

"Why are you convinced there's skulduggery afoot?"

"For one thing, that's not a word often heard in casual conversation." The corners of his mouth turned up. "For another, she didn't even tell her mom that she's moving away for Leonard."

"How do you know?"

"Because our mom is her mom's best friend and they had breakfast together. Our mom dropped by the house and I told her. She was shocked that Liv's mom hadn't said anything, because those two share everything. It's like he's a ghost. Like he doesn't exist."

Maggie was just taking a sip of tea and started to choke. He jumped up and took her mug, set it on the coffee table. Then he patted her back.

"Are you okay?"

"Fine." She looked up at him, eyes watering. "I'll get you another beer."

"I'm not finished with this one." He pointed a finger at her. "Don't move. Not until you tell me what you know about Leonard."

"What makes you think I know—"

He held up a hand. "Just stop. This is me. You can't fool anyone, let alone your big brother."

"Do you hear that?" She looked at the baby monitor. "I think Danielle is waking up. She's been teething and—"

"Classic deflection. My focus is legendary and you know I'm not that easily distracted. Come on, Mags. Give it up."

"Okay." Guilt was written all over her pretty face. "But you cannot tell Olivia that I'm the weak link."

"Promise. Now spill it." He sat back down on the couch and waited.

"Okay." She blew out a long breath. "But remember that Olivia gave notice that she was quitting twice before."

"It was her way of asking for a raise," he defended.

"No. It was her way of asking for *more*."

"More of what?"

"From life." Maggie shook her head. "I only say that because she needed Leonard to help her go through with leaving her job this time."

"I don't get it."

"For a smart guy, you can be awfully dense sometimes. She made up a fake boyfriend so you wouldn't give her a hard time about quitting and talk her into not doing it."

"I wouldn't do that," he defended.

"Really? Now who's being weird?" his sister said sarcastically.

Brady thought about the interviews Olivia had set up, all the lame excuses he'd used to avoid hiring her replacement. "Maybe I would a little. She's the best assistant I've ever had and I'll be lost without her."

"Well, get used to it. Leonard might be a figment of her imagination, but she really does have a job offer out of state. A terrific one."

He was surprised at the wave of relief he felt knowing that there wasn't a man she cared enough about to move for, but that didn't mean there wouldn't be retribution for trying to trick him. He just hadn't decided yet what form payback would take.

"Do you know where the job is?"

"California. It's in upper management in a start-up company. Someone she knows from college."

Damn. He could deal with an imaginary boyfriend, but this was about a professional opportunity that by all accounts was a really good offer. "I could promote her to upper management," he decided.

Maggie gave him a pitying look, as if he were dumb as dirt. "I know you'd like to make this about her career, Brady, but it's not. This is personal."

"I don't know what you're talking about."

"All right. If that's the way you want to play this." She sighed. "She has no life here—"

"How can you say that? She has a home. Family. Friends. You," he said holding out his hand to include her. "She has a terrific way of life."

"Brady, she's lonely. All I'm saying is give her a reason to stay."

"That's not a good idea." He knew what she meant and resisted with every fiber of his being. "Then everything changes. It gets complicated. I'd never do anything to hurt her. I already slipped up once and kissed her—"

"What?" Maggie's voice was sharp with attention. "You kissed Olivia?"

"It was nothing."

"How can a kiss be nothing?"

"She made a remark." He shrugged. "It was something about my reputation as not being much in the kissing department."

"Way to go, Liv," his sister murmured.

"What?"

"So the way to go was to kiss her and prove she was wrong?"

"Of course."

But he was the one who'd gotten it wrong. It had been a colossal miscalculation, because every time he saw her he wanted to kiss her again—upstairs in his bed.

"And it meant nothing to you?" Maggie's tone challenged him to deny the truth. "Kissing Olivia was like kissing the wall?"

"No. If I'm being honest—"

"Please."

"It was pretty awesome." There, he'd said it. Now he waited for Maggie to tell him he was seven ways a fool.

"So you didn't hate it." Maggie nodded thoughtfully. "Okay, I say again—give her a reason to stay. A seduction. It doesn't have to be complicated, just two consenting adults enjoying each other. No one has to fall in love or anything."

"Do you really think Olivia would go for that? She's a traditional woman."

"She is traditional. But she's a *woman,* if you get my drift. Take her out to dinner. A movie. Romance her. And before you bring up the L-word, look up the meaning of romance. Synonyms are story, tale, narrative."

"How do you know that?"

"I read a lot," she said wryly. "My point is, give her a great story. The two of you get it out of your system and move on just as you were before."

"I'll think about it."

The truth was that Brady liked his sister's point. Maggie was telling him that Olivia wanted a seduction. What a happy coincidence.

He would very much like to seduce her.

Chapter Eight

"So almost everyone in the company has RSVP'd and attendance at the employee weekend looks to be around eighty-five percent."

Olivia sat in the chair on the other side of Brady's desk as they discussed the upcoming company-wide event just a few weeks away.

"That's better than last year," he commented.

"It is."

And right after it ended she would be out of here. The thought evoked more sadness than exhilaration. She was going to miss this job, this office. The jade monkey on the bookshelf behind him caught her eye. He'd brought it back from a trip to China. The thing was ugly and she'd told him so, but she would miss that, too.

"Is something wrong, Liv?" Brady leaned back in his chair, squeezing the orange foam ball.

She looked out the window, where it was below freezing and the pewter-colored sky threatened snow. "It's gray and cloudy."

"I didn't think that bothered you."

Normally it didn't, but today that was her story and she was sticking to it. "I'm a little gloomy. Sorry about that. I'll try to perk up."

"Not on my account. You're allowed." He tossed the rubber ball from one hand to the other. "You still haven't told me where you're moving. Where the new job is. Where Leonard lives."

Was it her imagination, or was there just the slightest edge in his voice? If she were reading those last three words, would *Leonard* be italicized?

Then again, what did it really matter? And so what if he knew where she was going, because she'd still be gone.

She decided to ignore the opportunity to lie yet again about Leonard and focus on the truth for a change. "The job is in California. My friend from college, Colin Buchanan, is starting up a tech company in Santa Clarita, a suburb north of Los Angeles. It's not competition for you. Don't worry."

"I wasn't." He squeezed the orange ball until his knuckles turned white. "And what does Leonard do in California?"

She knew Brady was taking advantage of this momentary melancholy, a slight opening of the weakness window, in order to get the information she'd peevishly withheld. It was good strategy in business, but this strayed into personal territory. Even though Leonard wasn't real, this subject fell squarely under the heading "None of his concern."

"You know, Brady, we have a lot of work to do and not much time. Keeping busy is the best cure for my mood. I have a list of things that need to be done for the company's big weekend. At the top is a reminder to you. The employee of the year is your decision. Then there are bonuses. And also important is who you want to replace me. Do you need more interviews? I can expand my search parameters—"

He held up a hand to stop her. "Let's start with who's going to fill your shoes. I'd like the notes and work histories of your top three recommendations from the interviews I already conducted."

"All right. I'll get the file for you."

Finally, he was being a grown-up about this. Just as he'd promised. He was a man of his word. He meant what he said. So when he said marriage wasn't in his plans, one would be wise to take the message seriously.

Call her fickle, but Olivia liked it better when he was nitpicking job applicants and trying to talk her out of leaving.

She stood and walked through the doorway into her office, where the information he wanted was in with her active folders. She grabbed it and was ready to return when there was a beep from the security system indicating that someone had opened the front door.

Brady must have heard it, too, because he said from just behind her, "Do I have an appointment I don't know about?"

"There's nothing on the calendar. And your mom dropped by this morning with Danielle. As far as I know there's no crisis in my family. I have no idea—"

Then a tall, stunning redhead walked into the room. Shrugging out of her black quilted jacket, she said, "Hello, Brady. It's been a long time."

"Tiffani Guthrie." He didn't say more; he didn't move to greet the woman. He kept Olivia between them, almost as if he was taking cover behind her.

Beautiful cinnamon-colored eyes settled on Olivia for

a moment, then apparently gathered enough visual data to determine she wasn't a threat worthy to address.

Without a word, she returned her gaze to Brady. "How are you? You look well."

"I'm great. Heard you were back in town."

"Good news—and bad—travels fast in Blackwater Lake. It's nice to know some things don't change." She folded her jacket over her arm. "I'm not sure where I fall in the gossip spectrum. But I can guess. You didn't look me up."

It was a statement without whine or pout. Olivia really didn't want to be positive at all about this woman, but she had to give her a point for that.

"I didn't think we had anything more to say." Brady's voice was neutral, giving no clue about his feelings.

"I deserve that." Her sad smile drew attention to the fact that her lips were perfect, her mouth worthy of a magazine cosmetics ad. "Didn't you at least want to see how I held up? If the years had been kind? Whether or not I got fat and frumpy?"

On the surface, the question was designed to be self-effacing, but in reality it did two other things. Drew one's attention to a killer body that was flawlessly showcased in brown leather boots with four-inch heels, skintight jeans and a snug powder-blue sweater. The second thing she wanted to accomplish was hearing Brady pay her a compliment about her killer body. And if Olivia was being honest, the other woman deserved one. She was gorgeous.

Olivia braced herself, waiting for him to tell this woman that she was as beautiful as the last time he'd seen her. When she dumped him. His mother had directed her, Olivia, to run interference for him, but the order was unnecessary. She was feeling protective all on her own.

"So, Tiffani," she interjected before he could say anything. "Apparently Texas agrees with you."

"You're right, Liv. Well said." There was amusement in Brady's voice.

"It didn't turn out like I'd hoped." His old girlfriend didn't appear amused as she glanced around the richly decorated room. "But you're certainly doing all right for yourself. Everyone I talked to made sure to let me know how successful you are."

"I've been lucky."

When he moved closer to Tiffani, Olivia wanted to put out an arm to stop him, the instinctive reaction a driver had to protect the front-seat passenger when suddenly braking. She came close to telling him to stay behind her for his own safety, but managed to hold those words back.

Instead she said, "It's not all about luck when you have a good product, superior work ethic and make smart business decisions."

He glanced at her beside him, a united front. "I didn't do it by myself. Sharp, loyal employees make all the difference."

Tiffani's mouth pulled tight for a moment, then she glanced at Olivia. "You look familiar. Didn't we go to high school together?"

"Yes. I'm Olivia Lawson. You were two years ahead of me in school."

"Right. Now I remember. We took a business class together and you were adamant about finding success in the big city. I'm surprised you're still here in Blackwater Lake."

"And I'm surprised you're back in town," Brady said. "It seemed like you couldn't get away fast enough."

"I was young," she said. "And stupid, I admit it. I didn't see much future here after we broke up."

"That was your idea." Olivia kept her tone as calm and impersonal as possible, considering that inside she was shaking with anger. "And it didn't take you long to find someone else."

"Not my finest hour," she admitted. "But I thought I'd found what I wanted. It didn't work out. My only consolation is that I tried. I didn't just settle for a job here in Blackwater Lake. I wasn't mousy." Although it appeared the comment was self-directed, she was looking straight at Olivia when she said it.

Olivia wanted to fire back with "Who are you calling mousy?" but Brady went on the attack first.

"Olivia is the best executive assistant I've ever had and makes solid, proactive decisions." He took a step forward and the tension in his shoulders was obvious. "She's bright and beautiful and not dependent on a man who moves her to South Armpit, Texas, then proceeds to fall on his face."

"That pretty much sums up my life. And I wasn't putting Olivia down. Although you have no reason to believe that." Tiffani took a deep breath. "You're right about everything. I made a stupid decision going with Wes. The truth was I wanted to get away from Blackwater Lake, but I was afraid to do it on my own. Now I'm back. I'm here because I didn't want to run into you in public and have this conversation. It seemed better to do it in private." There was deep sadness in her eyes. "I'm sorry about the way I broke things off with you and I hope you're happy. Truly." She tried to smile. "There. The air is cleared and if we pass each other on Main Street, I hope we can be friendly."

"I'm sorry about going off like that." Brady's shoulders relaxed. "Thanks for coming here, Tiff. I'd like to be friends."

"Good. You, too, Olivia. Maybe we can go to lunch sometime."

"Maybe."

If we make it quick, Olivia thought, because she was the one leaving soon. This confrontation had not gone as expected, because she'd expected to thoroughly dislike this woman. But she really seemed to have changed.

"I'll see you out," Brady said.

He walked over to the other woman, who turned toward the front door. When they were gone, Olivia let out a long breath. The jury was out for now, but Tiffani Guthrie didn't seem like a complete witch.

The big news flash, though, was the way Brady had defended Olivia. Surely he wouldn't do that unless he cared. And he'd done it in spite of the fact that he believed she was moving away for a man, exactly what Tiffani had done.

Wait, wait, wait, she thought. The fact was that she wanted a husband and family and he didn't. As he'd told her sister, to hang on to a relationship was a waste of time when you had different life goals.

And just before Tiffani arrived he'd begun to take the steps to choose Olivia's replacement. He was being a grown-up, proving that he was a man of his word. It was wrong of her to wish he wasn't.

The words had just popped out of his mouth, Brady thought. Instinct to defend Olivia from Tiffani had kicked in. Everything he'd said was true: she was bright, beautiful and the best assistant in the history of assistants.

Since Tiffani had left, he'd been staring at his computer monitor and not focusing on it. That in itself was weird, because he could always focus and computers were easy to understand.

Unlike women.

He was still trying to wrap his mind around the fact that there was no Leonard. It was surprising how happy he was about that. Still, Olivia didn't know he knew she was lying. There must be a way to use it and get what he wanted, which was for her to stay. She'd made up a fake boyfriend so Brady couldn't talk her out of quitting. That must mean she didn't really want to go, because if she did she would. Right?

"Women are so complicated." He dragged his fingers through his hair. When there was a soft knock on his door he said, "Come in."

Olivia let herself into the room. She was wearing her black coat, leather gloves and a multicolored knit hat with a pom-pom on the top. She looked just about as cute as he'd ever seen her.

"Going home?"

She glanced toward the window. "That was the plan, but it's seriously snowing."

"Really?" He glanced outside and in the lights rimming the yard he saw big wet flakes coming down hard. It was practically a curtain of white. "Wow. When did it start? I didn't notice."

"Yeah. You tend to do that when you're involved in work."

It was a good thing she couldn't read his mind. "How are the roads? Did you check with the Blackwater Lake Department of Transportation for an update?"

"Yeah. No closures yet, but people are getting stuck. It's really slippery out there."

"Then you're not going out there." He got an image of her small compact car sliding off the road, down an embankment and into a ravine. "That's an order."

"Really?" She gave him a wry look. "I'm quitting in

a few weeks and you're snapping out commands like a pharaoh?"

He grinned. "I like the sound of that."

"Of course you do. Just keep in mind the toga and sandals are tough for any man to pull off, but especially during a rugged Montana winter."

"Good point." He stood and came around the desk. "Make fun all you want, but driving in this when it's not necessary isn't the smart thing to do. And I practically just finished telling Tiffani how intelligent you are."

She looked anxiously out the window. "There's no way to know how long it will last."

"Doesn't matter. Spend the night." The thought of her in one of his numerous guest rooms had far too much appeal. In his room would be even better, and the thought would never have occurred to him if he hadn't kissed her.

"I can't, Brady. I have to get home."

"Why?"

Two beats later she said, "Good question. There are no pets or people waiting."

He felt a pang of guilt about that. Being his assistant was tough because he was a demanding boss and that took a toll on a personal life.

"Look, Liv, it's my fault you didn't get out of here before the storm. I've given you a lot to do and there's a deadline. So, spend the night here. It's not like I don't have enough rooms to put up a small army. You'd be doing me a favor. Living with the guilt if something happened to you would be a crushing proposition." And here came the final argument. "It's not like you haven't stayed overnight here before."

Sometimes they'd worked late and had an early day the next morning, so she'd stayed over. It was convenient. But there was that one time when she'd showed up on his doorstep and said there was something she had to confess. Something she had to get off her chest. As it turned out, she fell asleep on the family-room sofa and never told him. He was still curious about what had been on her mind.

Olivia glanced out the window where, if possible, it was snowing harder. "Are you sure it's not a problem?"

No, he wasn't sure. After kissing her he wasn't sure about anything. But he didn't want her driving when it was dangerous.

"I'm positive," he said.

"All right, then. I guess I'll take my coat off and hang it up."

She shrugged out of it and he watched the sexy sway of her hips as she left the room. The prospect of having Olivia here in his house overnight was unexpected and exhilarating. Brady powered down his computer then turned out the lights in his office.

Making his way to the kitchen, he passed the entryway and noticed the fresh flowers on the circular table in the center. Nothing exotic—it was winter, after all—just carnations and baby's breath, but the floral fragrance was incredibly pleasant. He figured Olivia must be responsible for the comfortable, homey touch. What else besides her sexy walk and domestic touches had he deliberately not noticed about her?

In the kitchen he saw that she'd removed her navy crepe suit jacket and hung it on the back of a chair in the nook. She'd rolled up the silky sleeves of her white blouse and opened the refrigerator door.

"What's for dinner?" he asked.

There was a wry expression on her face when she straightened and glanced over her shoulder. "The plot thickens. You weren't really worried about me driving home in a snowstorm. It was all an elaborate scheme to get me to cook."

"You found me out." He slid his fingers into the front pockets of his jeans. "And since the blizzard is an integral part of this nefarious conspiracy, you should assume I have some serious skills."

"So noted."

"Now that that's settled, I'd still like to know what you're planning for dinner. Also, I just realized that I'm starving. Is there anything to eat in this house?"

"Fortunately your brilliant assistant—"

"And beautiful." Might as well get his quote accurate. That cat was already out of the bag.

"Whatever." She waved her hand dismissively. "Your assistant makes sure that the housekeeper stocks your refrigerator and pantry with all of your favorite foods, and some that are even healthy for you."

Brady leaned his back against the granite-covered island across from the cooktop and refrigerator where she was standing. He liked being with her in the kitchen. He enjoyed everything about it, especially the carefree smile on her face and the sparkle in her pretty blue eyes. It made him wistful, wishing he did have the skills to conjure a snowstorm at quitting time just to keep her there.

At least until she moved away.

"And is there wine to go with this sumptuous feast?" he asked.

"As it happens there is. One of my favorites."

"Imagine that, what with you stocking the place and all."

She directed his attention to the climate-controlled refrigerator where he stored his wine. "There's a lovely Cabernet on the top shelf. Your job is to open the bottle so it can breathe."

"Okay. But it has to be said, you're awfully bossy."

"I delegate. There's a difference. And it's one of my best qualities."

Just then she turned, giving him the best seat in the house from which to observe her impressive resources. Very nice posterior. From his perspective, delegating was *not* her best asset.

Brady opened the wine and set it on the table, then put out glasses, plates, napkins and eating utensils. Behind him he heard the microwave humming, pots banging and water turned on at the sink. Olivia made a salad and handed it to him to put by their place settings.

Into a saucepan she poured a plastic container of soup that she'd bought at the specialty grocery store in town. No canned stuff for him. After that she buttered slices of bread, added cheese and ham, then put the sandwiches in a frying pan on the cooktop.

"Voilà. A hot and hearty meal." Turning, she saw him watching her and smiled. "It's nothing fancy, but it's filling and nutritious."

"This bachelor is pathetically grateful for you throwing something together."

"You're welcome. Why don't you pour the wine and we can start with our salad."

He did as she asked, then held the chair for her to sit. It could have been imagination or a trick of the lighting, but he swore her cheeks blushed a pretty pink. For the next hour they talked, laughed and polished off the bottle of wine. Brady was feeling kind of perfect as they cleaned up the kitchen together.

Then a weird feeling came over him. They spent hours working together during the day and had done so for the last five years. There was a routine. Work. She went home, he stayed here alone—unless he had female company.

But he suddenly realized that everything with Olivia was different since he'd kissed her. For one thing, this house had never seemed so big and lonely before. Having her here now made him aware of just how alone he felt when she was gone.

They were standing in front of the sink, where she was washing the frying pan, and he waited for her to hand it over to be dried. All he could think about was pulling her against him and kissing her. In a few weeks she'd be gone and so would the temptation. There was something he was curious about and if he wanted an answer, now was the time.

"Liv, do you remember that night you dropped by spontaneously? You said you had something to tell me and it couldn't wait until Monday?"

"What?" She blinked at him like a deer caught in headlights. The surprise was just as stark and real as when he'd broken off that unexpected and spectacular kiss.

"You remember. You'd been out for a girls' night with Sydney McKnight. She was the designated driver and dropped you off because you insisted on talking to me."

She'd had a little too much girls' night out and told him that her friend had tried to talk her out of dropping by. But she was adamant that it was way past time to tell him what was on her mind. Some instinct told him nothing would be the same if she did, so Brady hadn't pushed it that night. Afterward he figured ignorance was bliss, but not so much now.

"What did you want to say to me?" he asked, drying the pan she handed over.

She took longer than necessary to dry her hands on the dish towel and fold it, setting it beside the sink. Shrugging, she said, "I don't remember."

But she wouldn't meet his gaze.

"You recall spending the night," he prompted.

"Not really." She glanced around the kitchen, checking to see that everything was tidy. And still avoided looking at him.

Brady didn't believe her. In spite of pulling off the Leonard story for a while, she wasn't a very good liar. She'd fallen asleep on the sofa and he'd carried her upstairs, put her to bed.

Tonight he wanted to *take* her to bed—his bed.

Now she looked at him. "I'm really tired. It's been a long day. I think I'll go up. My usual room?"

With every ounce of testosterone in his body he wanted to say, *no, my room.* Somehow he held back. "Yeah."

"Good night, Brady. See you tomorrow."

That's what she said every evening before heading home, but this time he wanted more.

He threw his dish towel on the counter and swore in frustration. He went to the wet bar in the family room and grabbed a bottle of scotch. After opening it, he poured some into a tumbler then tossed it back.

Change was never good. He hated it and couldn't seem to stop what was happening now. Because he'd kissed Olivia. The thing was, he wasn't the kind of guy who would hit on a woman committed to another man. But she wasn't, really.

What if he romanced her, just to out her on the fake boyfriend? If he could get her to admit it, they could have a serious discussion about the fact that she didn't really want to leave. This was his good deed, saving her from herself.

It was a plan, and in his opinion a good one. Tomorrow he would put it into action.

Chapter Nine

"So, what are you cooking for breakfast?"

Olivia closed the refrigerator and turned to look at Brady who was showered, dressed and smelling like the sexiest possible combination of spice and sin. Her pulse started to race and her knees literally got weak. Whatever cologne he used should be illegal on account of it giving him an unfair advantage.

"I already made a pot of coffee." She knew this was token resistance because he always got his way. "Didn't we go through this last night?"

"We did." He folded his arms over his chest. "You are my beautiful, brilliant assistant and I have skills to control the weather in order to get you to cook."

"Technically that's what we talked about, but—"

"What?"

"I really need to go home and change." She was wearing stuff she'd borrowed from him that made her look as sexy as a sack of potatoes. "I need to get ready for work."

He leaned a broad shoulder against the wall just inside the doorway. "There are two problems with that idea. One: your boss doesn't care if you wear sweatpants too big for you and an equally oversized T-shirt."

"What's the second problem?"

"The roads haven't been plowed yet. You know as well as I do that out here by the lake is the last place to get cleared."

"Oh."

"Therefore, I repeat—what's for breakfast?"

"What do you do when you're alone?"

"Pop-Tarts."

"Seriously?"

"I know, right?" He grinned. "You might want to be proactive in this whole process of healthier eating. It would be very helpful."

Trying to keep a straight face, Olivia stared at him. "Number one—you're the host. Number two—that makes it your responsibility to plan the menu and prepare provisions. Something nutritious."

"I can do that," he said cheerfully.

It struck her as a little odd how cheerful he was, considering he'd been such a gloomy pain in the neck since she'd given her notice. Maybe he was reconciled to the inevitable. But he could be a little less enthusiastically cheerful, she thought peevishly.

"You should make omelets," she suggested. "And before you say no, I know you can do it."

He'd made a really good breakfast that time she'd dropped by unannounced—when she'd had the terrible idea to tell him exactly how she felt about him. But he'd given her a glass of wine and on top of what she'd had with Sydney, she fell asleep before spilling her guts. A good thing, too. Work would have been awkward and she'd probably have lost his friendship. When the buzz wore off, she'd realized that was a risk she wasn't willing to take.

"Omelets coming up." He moved in front of the cooktop. "Mushrooms, tomato, spinach and cheese?"

That was what they both liked. "I'll cut everything up."

"And make toast?" He reached up and easily retrieved the shallow, curved stainless steel pan from the hanging rack over the kitchen island.

All of her feminine parts quivered and sighed as she watched him. "Yes, I can do toast. But that means you set the table."

"Deal."

She blinked at him. "That was too easy."

"I'm sure I don't know what you mean." He had the fridge open and was bending over to pull the vegetables out of the crisper.

Olivia wasn't sure she'd ever noticed before what an awesome butt he had. And that's when she realized things were not the same. When she'd spent the night at his house before, they'd always sparred over division of chores involved with food preparation and cleanup. Before, the banter had always been easy and comfortable. This morning was different and complicated.

It was because of that kiss. She'd always had a crush on Brady, but it had gone to the next level the moment his lips touched hers.

"What was too easy?" He set tomato, mushrooms and spinach on the island, then handed her a knife and cutting board.

"You agreed to cook and set the table." She shrugged. "Normally there's more negotiation and I end up doing most of the work."

"I help clean up," he protested.

"Telling me where everything goes doesn't qualify as actually exerting yourself."

"Wow." He looked at her, then cracked eggs into a bowl. "Someone woke up on the crabby side of the bed. That was downright surly."

"Not by a long shot." She took a tomato and diced it up, perhaps using a little more force than was necessary.

"All evidence to the contrary."

"Since when do you notice what kind of mood I'm in?"

"I always do." He added milk to the eggs and whipped them with a wire whisk. "It just doesn't always require me to make a comment."

"Today is different?" Maybe she wasn't the only one who'd noticed.

"Yes, it is. Because I'm trying to make your last few weeks as my assistant as pleasant as possible."

She was a little skeptical of his sincerity, but her parents had brought her up to always be gracious. "That's very nice of you."

"I'm a very nice guy."

And humble, too, she wanted to say, but she knew that wasn't being fair. He *was* a nice guy. It's just that spending the night with him—scratch that, sleeping in his house—had brought out deeply buried feelings, then teased her with everything she'd ever wanted and would never have. That's why she was leaving. Why was it that the smart and rational move turned her into a sarcastic witch?

"Veggies and cheese are ready," she told him. "I'll make the toast. Wheat?"

"You're reading my mind." He was setting out plates, napkins and eating utensils. "I'll do the eggs now."

She popped bread into his four-slice toaster then watched him cook. At just the right moment he scraped the vegetables and cheese onto the eggs then expertly folded it over.

"You're very good at that," she said.

"I'm very good at a lot of things." He glanced over his shoulder and there was a roguish look in his eyes.

He probably made omelets for his overnight female guests all the time. Olivia had seen the evidence, what with working in his house. Forgotten lipstick. Undergarments made of satin and lace. Girl stuff. She had no right to be jealous but that never stopped her before. Until now she'd never commented in an effort not to compromise their working relationship. But now she had nothing to lose.

She leaned her elbows on the granite-topped island and rested her chin in her hands. "I guess you've had a lot of practice cooking for the women who spent the night here."

He met her gaze, one dark eyebrow raised. "Why, Miss Lawson, are you jealous?"

"Nope. Curious."

"Actually, my mother made sure I knew how to make basic things so I wouldn't starve or eat junk. It was her philosophy that boys should know how to take care of themselves and not live in an environment that the health department would condemn."

"Your mother is a smart woman."

"I think so, too." He cut the omelet with the spatula and put half on each plate.

She buttered the toast and added that to the eggs and they grabbed the food and took it to the table.

"I'll pour the coffee," she said.

"That would be great." He sat down with his back to the window that looked out on the majestic, snow-covered mountains. "Just so we both agree you volunteered and I'm not a male sexist pig."

"So stipulated." She laughed even while wishing his charm was less potent. "I guess you dusted off your sensitivity chip, because it's intact and functioning today."

She retrieved two mugs from the cupboard. After filling them, she set one beside each of their plates then brought sweetener and cream to the table.

Brady stirred both into the dark, steaming liquid, then took a sip. "You make the best coffee, Liv. At the risk of being that obnoxious, overbearing boss, it would mean a lot to me if you would pass along the secret to your replacement."

"So you've moved past anger and denial and are settling into acceptance of the situation?"

"Do I have a choice?"

"Not really, no." Again she noticed the lack of annoyance and pouting on his part. It was very uncharacteristic and disconcerting.

"That reminds me," he said. "I'd like to take you out to dinner."

"What?" She was about to take another sip of coffee. If his timing had been just a little different, she would have choked on it. "Why?"

"Why not?"

"Because you're…you," she said lamely.

"And your point?"

"You're the boss. Oh, I get it. This is a working dinner."

"No."

"Then I don't get it." She stared at him, trying to figure out what was going through his mind.

"There's nothing to get. Can't I take my assistant out for a nice dinner?"

"You never have before." Just when she'd thought it was safe to let down her guard.

"Sure I have."

She shook her head. "There were meals out that you paid for, but work was always involved. What are you up to, Brady?"

"Wow." He took a bite of eggs and chewed, his gaze locked on hers. "Feel the love."

No. She didn't want to. Not anymore. "This isn't like you."

"How do you know? This is the first time you quit."

"It's actually the third time, but who's counting? You never believed me before."

He set his fork down on his plate. "Look, if you're right, and I'm sure you are, it's about time I treated you to a nice, leisurely dinner before you leave. No work talk allowed. After all, they say third time's the charm."

"I don't know about this—"

"Come on, Liv. Just say yes. You know I'll get my way eventually. I always do."

That was true; it's why she'd made up a boyfriend. Only a lie would get her out of this gracefully, and how graceful was that? "All right. That would be very nice."

"Great. Tonight." He wiped his mouth with a napkin and stood up. "I have work to do."

"Okay. I'll do the dishes." She started to stand.

"Finish your breakfast. And leave this for the housekeeper." Just before walking out of the room, he stopped and looked at her. "I'll pick you up at seven. Wear a nice little black dress."

Before she could protest, he was gone. She stared at the empty doorway, wondering what just happened.

"You're up to something, Brady O'Keefe. What game are you playing?"

Pretend boyfriends were so much easier to understand.

That evening, Brady pulled his car to a stop outside of Olivia's apartment building while nursing a high level of anticipation for seeing her in a little black dress. Did she have any clue how cute she'd looked wearing his clothes that morning? It wouldn't have bothered him if she'd lost the sweats, letting him get a good look at her legs. He'd seen them before when she wore skirts, but he'd have liked to see more. They were pretty spectacular legs. The T-shirt would have covered other stuff he was curious about, but…

Now the best he could hope for was her taking his suggestion about the little black dress. Especially because he'd feel kind of stupid in this suit and tie if she was in jeans.

After looking at his watch and noting it was 6:59, he opened the door of his SUV. After the snowstorm, he'd decided it would hold the road better than the sports car. The cold air hit him like a block of ice and he could see his breath. When Olivia moved to California, would she miss Montana winters? Or would she be relieved to be out of here?

Away from him.

Brady walked briskly up the sidewalk. It had been a while since he'd come to her place and past visits had probably been work-related. This was about work, too, having everything to do with maintaining his well-organized business environment.

The sidewalk had been salted so as not to be slippery and the pellets crunched under his shoes. Except for the walkway, snow covered the ground on the path to apartment number ten.

Outside her door was a large red clay pot filled with potting soil and a dead plant he couldn't identify. Stuck in the dirt was a wrought-iron stand holding a flag that said Welcome Friends.

Brady figured he fell into that category and knocked. The door opened almost immediately, and he got his answer to the question of her attire. She'd taken his suggestion and looked more amazing than he'd ever seen her look.

The dress was high necked, long sleeved and all lace. The skirt was short enough to let him see more of her legs than he ever had before. Instead of satisfying his curiosity, it just made him want to check out the view all the way up. And then there were the smoky, silky black nylons she was wearing with mile-high patent leather heels.

He nearly swallowed his tongue, which made it kind of impossible to say anything, but fortunately his eyes were working just fine.

Olivia frowned. "Brady? Are you okay?"

"Yeah. It's just—" There really was no way to explain this reaction, so he said, "It's cold out here."

"Oh. Right. Come in." She stepped back and pulled the door wide.

"I'd forgotten how nice this place was," he said, looking around.

"Thanks. I've been pretty happy here."

He liked the cozy living room with its green-coral-and-beige floral-patterned sofa and two striped club chairs done in coordinating colors. The grouping was arranged in front of the fireplace, where the gas log was lit. Dark wood end tables bracketed the couch and a sofa table behind it held family photos—her parents, sister. No one else. And that gave him his opening.

He walked over and examined the scattered pictures. "I don't see any of Leonard." There was silence behind him and he turned to look at her expression, making his own blank and innocent, yet inquisitive and interested. "How come?"

"Really? I thought there was one of him here." She moved slowly, studying each photo. Probably trying to come up with a plausible excuse for not having one of the man she was supposedly moving to be with. "Hmm. Guess not. I must have put it in the bedroom."

"Would you mind if I take a look?" His shrug was casual. "Shoot me for being curious, but I'd really like to see what the guy who's taking you away from me looks like."

When he moved toward the hallway that led to the two bedrooms, she put a hand on his arm. "Brady, no." There was an edge in her voice that was just this side of panic.

"Just a quick peek?"

"Please don't. My room is a mess and that's embarrassing."

"I'm shocked and appalled. Überorganized, a-place-for-everything-and-everything-in-its-place Miss Olivia Lawson didn't tidy up her room?"

"Right? I have a reputation to maintain." Her smile was forced. "And it didn't seem necessary to straighten everything, since no one's going in there."

He couldn't look away from the stunning vision in black lace and thought how much he'd like to be in her room, getting her out of that dress. Her hair was pulled into a simple ponytail and she wore a black velvet headband as the only accessory, which somehow made her more elegant. Almost more than his next breath he wanted to loosen her hair and run his fingers through the silk of it.

But this was *not* why he'd come here. It was confirmation of why he didn't let himself feel this way. The business he'd worked so hard to build was going well and Olivia was an integral part of that. Everything in his life was clicking along smoothly and he wanted to keep it that way. That's why he was here.

On top of that, she'd pulled a fast one and now it was his turn to have a little fun.

"So, you clean up the bedroom when Leonard comes for a visit?"

"Seems like the polite thing to do when one has an overnight guest."

That was vague and not really an answer. So he asked more directly. "Has he ever been here to see you in your natural habitat?"

"No. He's pretty busy. It's hard for him to get away."

"So you go to see him?"

"Oh, you know. It's not easy to get anywhere from Blackwater Lake. The airport is so far away. Weekends are by definition pretty short..." She shrugged. "Aren't you hungry? I'm starving. I'll just get my coat."

Not very smooth, Liv. She pretty much sucked at lying.

Brady was about to challenge her flimsy explanation for not visiting Leonard, but she turned away and the electrical activity in his brain shorted out when he saw the back of her dress for the first time. And with good reason.

There was no back.

The lace formed a deep V, showing nothing but smooth, silky skin. At the top of a very long and sexy list of questions, not the least of which was how she would taste at that intriguing spot just above the waist, was what she was—or wasn't—wearing underneath.

While he was attempting to jump-start rational thought, she'd put on her fitted black coat and grabbed a small satin clutch purse.

"Okay, I'm ready."

"Good. Let's go." He put his hand at the small of her back to exit the apartment.

It wasn't safe to be here alone another minute. If they didn't get the hell out, he'd kiss her again and that wasn't part of his plan.

A short time later they were seated in the five-star res-

taurant at Blackwater Lake Lodge. It was a weeknight,
which, combined with the cold weather, explained the
lack of a crowd. Only two other couples were there and
Brady asked the hostess to seat them at the table in front
of the fireplace, where gentle flames danced. He ordered
an expensive bottle of wine, which he happened to know
was Olivia's favorite. A glass of the red for each of them
had just been poured by their waiter, who left them with
menus.

Brady picked up his glass. "I propose a toast."

"Okay. To what?"

"You and Leonard."

Her eyes narrowed slightly and her lips pulled tight,
but she touched her glass to his. Without a word, she took
a generous sip.

He studied her in the subdued lighting—the curve of
her cheek, full lips, big eyes—and thought she was the
most beautiful woman he'd ever seen. And he wanted her
bad. The challenge to focus on his mission was getting
more difficult because the ambience in this place was far
too romantic. It was like foreplay. He'd only chosen it because it was her favorite.

"So, do you and Leonard have a restaurant that's 'your'
place?"

"No." She folded her hands in her lap. "He likes pretty
much everything I do."

"He sounds easygoing," Brady persisted.

"He is." Her smile was tense. "We get along extremely
well together."

"It doesn't seem like you manage to carve out very
much couple time," he felt obligated to point out. "How
does Leonard keep the romance alive?"

"It takes two." She sipped her wine and didn't meet his

gaze. "Both people in a relationship are responsible for making it strong."

"That's true. And I have to hand it to you and Leonard for maintaining a loving bond. How do you deal with the long distance?"

"Wow, where to start…" She blew out a long breath. "We talk every day. Preferably Skype. Text a lot. You get a surprising amount of information that way."

It wouldn't work for him. Not long-term. He'd want to touch Olivia. Fold her in his arms. "Intimacy in the electronic age. Gotta love it."

"Yes." She picked up her menu and studied the items as if it was the most fascinating reading. "What do you like here?"

Way to change the subject, Liv. It was probably time to back off. For now.

"Let's see." He glanced at the choices as he always did, but more often than not he came back to the same thing. "The filet. It's better than I've had anywhere."

"Medium rare," they said together.

She laughed and added, "It's my favorite, too."

"To favorites," he said and picked up his wineglass again. "You're my favorite executive assistant and always will be."

"You don't know that, Brady. Whoever my replacement is will probably run circles around me. You'll be sorry you didn't let me go a long time ago."

"Do you regret it? Staying here in Blackwater Lake, I mean?"

Her expression grew pensive and just this side of sad. "I'm not sure. Sometimes I wonder if it was just easier to stay. Status quo is safer than the unknown."

"I know what you mean." And he really did. Every time his life changed, it wasn't a good thing. And he didn't like seeing her melancholy, so he completely changed the subject. "How is your sister doing?"

"Breaking up with Greg was the best thing for her." She pulled her gaze from the menu. "What you said to her certainly made an impression. One of the other teachers asked her out and apparently Greg didn't like it. He tried to tell her he'd been hasty and suggested they try a reconciliation."

"Apparently it didn't happen?"

"She told him time was precious and she wasn't wasting any more on him."

Her happy smile scratched open a dark place deep inside him and Brady felt a little desperation leak out. "Would Leonard be jealous of you having dinner with another man?"

"That's a good question." She tapped her lip. "I'm pretty sure he's not the jealous type."

"He should be." Brady couldn't keep his voice neutral. No matter how hard he tried to make it teasing, intensity wrapped around every word. "If you were mine, I wouldn't want you out with anyone but me."

Chapter Ten

On the drive from the restaurant back to her apartment, Olivia couldn't get Brady's words out of her mind.

If you were mine, I wouldn't want you out with anyone but me.

Of course he didn't mean *her*. He was talking in general terms about any woman he was dating. But the intensity in his eyes...for a split second, it had felt as if he was speaking directly to her.

"It's awful quiet over there." With one hand, Brady turned the steering wheel and guided the car into a parking place right outside her building. "Is something on your mind?"

"Yes." She met his gaze and resolved the lies she'd told were absolutely necessary to protect her soul. "I had a really nice time tonight."

"I'm glad. Me, too."

They sat there for several moments, smiling at each

other. It would be so easy to lean in, let body language ask for the kiss she wished for. But she didn't. She needed him to make the move so she would know he wanted it, too.

When he didn't move, she opened the car door. "Thanks for dinner, Brady. It was great. See you in the morning."

"Wait. I'll walk you to your door."

"That's not necessary." She was torn between wanting to spend every possible second with him and making a clean break. "It's freezing out."

"I wasn't raised by wolves. A gentleman always sees a lady safely inside."

"It's right there." She gestured toward her quiet building just a few feet away. "If the serial killer is inside, I'll give you the high sign."

"Nope. Not good enough. O'Keefe men have the highest standards."

"That's gentlemanly of you." If he ever decided to make a commitment, the chosen lady would be very lucky.

She crossed her fingers, praying that he didn't ask if Leonard walked her to the door. She was running out of evasive answers that weren't out-and-out falsehoods.

Fortunately he didn't inquire and she got out of the car and closed the door. No sense letting the warm air escape. He did the same, then met her on the sidewalk where they moved together up the path. Snow had melted during the day when it was sunny, but residual moisture froze when night fell. It was tricky navigating in four-inch heels and she slipped, would have gone down hard if Brady hadn't caught her.

"Thanks," she said breathlessly.

"You should have worn boots."

"Not with this dress."

"Yeah." His voice was hoarse and he tightened his arm around her, nestling her securely against his chest.

The outside light beside her door revealed his expression, showing something like heat in his eyes. It could have been her imagination, but that didn't stop the warmth sliding around deep down inside her. Then his head lowered, just a fraction. At least she thought so, because she was convinced that he would finally kiss her with full-on body-to-body contact, like that day in his office.

But she was wrong.

"Let's get you inside," he said.

Because he had the high standards of a gentleman, he kept his arm around her until they stood right in front of her door. "Here you are. Safe and sound."

Except for her hope. It was in harm's way and utterly defenseless.

"Thanks again for dinner."

"My pleasure. Good night, Liv." This time there was no doubt he lowered his head, because he gave her a friendly peck on the cheek. "See you in the morning."

"Bright and early."

She unlocked her door and stepped inside, watching him walk back to his car. He waved one last time, then got inside and drove away. Once again she felt as if her heart had been kicked to the curb.

The worst part was she couldn't even get mad. It wasn't as if he'd promised anything, but hope had a way of being knocked down and still getting back up. Now it was clear that tonight's fancy dinner was just Brady being more subtle about convincing her not to quit. All it did was underscore that moving away from him was the only way to preserve her innate faith, hope and optimism. The only way to keep that part of herself from flickering out forever.

She didn't want to be a dried-up, bitter old maid.

Her gaze fell on the message hanging from the stand in her clay pot. "Welcome friends, my backside."

She was burning that flag before she moved to California.

The next morning Olivia was grumpy and tired. That's what happened when you tossed, turned and dreamed of a kiss that never happened.

She pulled into Brady's semicircular driveway and parked in her usual place. After exiting the car, she walked up the steps to the oval-etched glass front door. This was the same routine she'd had every workday for the last five years, but now her enthusiasm was just gone.

The time was fast approaching when her agreement with Brady would be fulfilled. Two more weeks until the employees who worked remotely would be in town. When that was over, she'd be out of there. Her replacement had been hired. Brady picked Shelly Shows, the lady in plaid who wanted to work closer to home. She was starting next week. Then Olivia would go.

It was a sobering thought and put her in a mood—one she had to hide from Brady. He would use it against her. There wasn't a doubt in her mind about that, because she didn't for one minute believe he had given in and gracefully accepted her resignation. That wasn't ego talking, just that she knew him really well.

There was a security system beep when she opened the front door and stepped inside. He would have heard it, too, and would be waiting for her, ready to give orders and a list of things to do. With a heavy heart, she walked through the house and down the hall to the business wing.

She walked into her office and there was something waiting, all right, but it wasn't Brady.

A bouquet bigger than a Smart car was sitting on her

desk. Bright yellow, orange and purple flowers cheerfully greeted her and she had the most absurd urge to cry. There was a small white envelope with her name on it stuck into the plastic pitchfork thing that florists used to display the sender's message. Probably she should see what it said.

She stepped in front of her desk and dropped her purse on top, then plucked out the white card. There was a happy face and it was simply signed, "Brady."

How very sweet. And incredibly annoying.

Olivia looked at his closed door and headed straight for it as anger won out over squishy, tender feelings. She knocked once and opened it, not waiting for permission to enter.

She marched over to his desk and announced, "It's not going to work."

"What?" He pulled his attention away from the computer monitor and swiveled toward her. "Something's not working?"

"Oh, yeah." She jammed her fists on her hips. "Not working big-time."

"Care to enlighten me?" He picked up the orange squeeze ball and his fingers crushed it into his palm.

She took grim satisfaction in the fact that she planned to give him an earful and a whole lot to think about.

"I'm not changing my mind about leaving this job. And there's nothing you can do about that."

"You've made that clear."

"Have I?"

"Yes. I might be slow, but the message sank in that you're moving to California to be with Leonard. I've accepted your decision."

She heard the words but the tone lacked conviction and sincerity. "So why the bouquet?"

"I just thought you should know how I feel, and nothing says you're appreciated like flowers."

"And nothing says it's not going to change my mind like the words *no matter what you do I'm not changing my mind.*"

"Oh." He sat up straighter in his chair. "I get it. You think it's a bribe to convince you to stay."

"Of course I do."

"It's not. Trust me."

"Maybe that would happen if I didn't know you so well. This is so typical."

"That's harsh."

"But true. You'd do almost anything to keep from having your routine disrupted."

"I'll admit that I was resistant at first. And it's no secret that I dislike change, but sometimes that can't be helped."

She stared at him for several moments, not trusting the innocent expression on his handsome face. "So, why the flowers?"

"Just to let you know how much I appreciate all your hard work over the years."

"I've never received flowers before." This had incentive, persuasion, dangling carrot written all over it.

"Really?" His brows drew together. "This is the first time?"

It was a question without a good answer. If she told the truth and said no, he'd make some crack about Leonard being a slacker. "That's not the point."

"Seems like it to me. This isn't the reaction I expected from you."

"And what did you expect?" she asked.

"Maybe a heartfelt thank-you for the beautiful bouquet and sincere gesture of gratitude for all you've done for me and O'Keefe Technology."

"You're impossible." That was the best comeback she could manage, because guilt for possibly misjudging him was starting to creep in.

"You cut me to the quick," he said. "I just wanted to let you know that you're my friend. Whether you're here in Blackwater Lake, or living in California, you always will be my friend."

His words made her feel slimy and stupid. The word *fool* also came to mind. Also *ungrateful*. After a sleepless night of thinking about the kiss she'd wanted from him and the one he'd given her, *friend* was not the word to sweeten her disposition.

For the rest of the morning, Brady had left her alone. But later in the afternoon she sat in his office, briefing him on details for employee-appreciation weekend. She had the high points jotted down on a legal pad and checked them off one by one.

"I've reserved a block of rooms at Blackwater Lake Lodge. The number is based on the RSVPs received with a couple extra on hold, just in case. Also there's a deposit for conference rooms for Saturday's workshops. I've contacted speakers whose focus is on wellness in the workplace."

Brady got up and started pacing in front of the fireplace. "What about the awards dinner?"

"I've contracted with the manager of Fireside. The restaurant will be closed to the public that night for our private function. It will be the Lodge's responsibility to notify their guests of any possible inconvenience and recommend other places in town for their dining pleasure. I'm sure the Grizzly Bear Diner will be happy about it."

"No doubt. Any push back from the Lodge on this?"

She shook her head. "You make it worth their while."

"Do I?" He stopped for a moment and raised an eyebrow. "Yes, indeed."

Brady was a really fair and astute businessman and everyone was happy to accommodate him. He was also a good boss, she thought, and felt bad for giving him a hard time about the flowers.

"Besides," she continued, "it's not a holiday weekend and traditionally slow at the Lodge this time of year. They're happy to have us."

Soon she wouldn't be part of the "us."

"It sounds like everything is under control. Thank you, Olivia, for agreeing to stay on and handle this for me."

"Don't mention it." If she was being honest with herself, she would admit to being glad for the excuse to delay her departure a little longer. She stood. "So, if it's all right with you, I'm going to leave a little early and go shopping. Someone has to buy those traditional gifts for banquet night."

"What kind of stuff did you have in mind?"

"The usual for the honorees. Electronics. Everything from e-readers to phones, tablets and TVs."

"You might need some help with it."

She shook her head. "I've got the company credit card and Blackwater Lake Electronics will deliver everything to the Lodge for the awards banquet."

In the five years she'd been here, not once had he considered that she needed assistance. He'd never questioned her ability to handle the job.

"Don't worry about me. I'll be fine. Just wanted to make sure you didn't mind that I leave a little early."

"Not only do I not mind, I'm coming with you."

She should have tried to talk him out of it, but all of a sudden, the chore she'd been dreading didn't seem so bad. "You can get away?"

"Of course. I'm the boss."

She just didn't have the reserves to talk him out of it. "Okay. Let's go."

He drove to downtown Blackwater Lake, which was just fine with Olivia. She loved riding in his SUV. The sports car was fun, but in a guy way. She enjoyed the luxury in the bigger vehicle, especially the warmer in the butter-soft beige leather seat. The dashboard looked as though it belonged in a jet airplane and not for the first time she thought that people with money really were different. At least their cars were.

Still, with all his success, Brady hadn't changed in all the time she'd known him. He was still the same good-looking charmer who would never notice her the way she wanted him to. If friendship was all she could have, she'd enjoy it until the day Blackwater Lake was reflected in her rearview mirror.

He pulled the SUV to a stop at the curb in front of the store on Main Street. Staring at the signs in the big window, he said, "It doesn't get much better than this. A convenient parking place and a huge sale."

"Kind of brings a tear to your eye, doesn't it?"

"Just saying…" He grinned. "Okay, let's do this."

They exited the car and walked inside. Olivia knew the place was bigger than it looked from the outside. The interior was deep and filled with enough merchandise to make a geek's heart go pitter-patter. Overhead signs identified the various departments: phones in front; tablets, readers and laptops in the center; televisions in the back corner where an area was set up with reclining chairs in front of a very large flat-screen TV and home theater.

Before Brady could beeline for it, the store's owner walked up to them. Clark Gibson was somewhere in his late fifties to early sixties with gray hair and blue eyes. He was tall, trim and fit.

Holding out his hand he said, "Brady O'Keefe. It's been a long time."

"Hi, Mr. G."

"How are you, son?"

"Good. Yourself?"

"Can't complain. Jeff was here over the holidays."

Brady had been friends with Jeff Gibson in high school. "How does he like Seattle?"

"A lot of rain, but he's adjusting. Got a good job with Amazon. Proposed to his girl on New Year's Eve. We like her a lot. 'Bout time those two took the plunge."

"That's great." He shook his head. "I can't believe Jeff's getting married. The next time you talk to him, please give him my congratulations."

"Will do." The older man studied him and smiled. "You must hear this all the time, but you look just like your dad."

"I consider that a compliment, sir." There was a soft reverence in Brady's voice.

"Good. I meant it that way. He was a good man, good friend." The older man looked at Olivia. "And what's this I hear about you leaving town, young lady?"

"I know, right?" The sudden switch in conversational gears made her feel as if she had whiplash. "A job opportunity came my way in California and I couldn't pass it up."

Mr. Gibson nudged Brady. "You didn't make her an offer she couldn't refuse?"

"The Golden State has more perks than I could compete with," he answered.

"Seems like I heard that. A man?" Blue eyes twinkled. "Is it serious?"

"Could be." If Leonard existed. Olivia found it hard not to squirm while fibbing to this good-natured man.

"I'm glad for you," he said. "But I sure do wish you didn't have to move away."

"You and me both," Brady said, giving Olivia a funny look.

"Your folks will miss you."

"And I'll miss them. But you do what you have to." She shrugged and decided it was time to do what they came here for. "So, it's time for the annual O'Keefe Technology weekend bash and we came to shop."

"Excellent. I guess you know your way around." During the conversation he'd been glancing at customers browsing the aisles. "If you'll excuse me, I see someone who needs help."

"Thanks, Mr. G." Olivia looked to the left and right, getting her bearings. "Let's start with the tablets. Everyone likes those and they always want the latest version."

"Okay."

There was something in Brady's voice that Olivia couldn't define. But he seemed a little down and that surprised her. This stuff was right up his alley and he should be quivering with excitement. Then she checked herself. Monitoring his mood wasn't in her job description.

She turned to the long display table and they slowly walked along it, browsing the current devices, comparing features and price. After a spirited discussion, agreement was reached about which one to purchase and how many. She wrote down the pertinent numbers and later when the list was complete, she'd grab one of the salespeople and make his day.

When she looked up, Brady was still holding the tablet of choice and he had an odd expression on his face, equal parts distant and sad.

She knew ignoring it would be wise, but she simply couldn't. "Okay, talk to me."

He looked up and met her gaze. "About?"

"What's bugging you?" She recognized the look on his face, the one he got when he planned to tell her she was imagining things. It would save time if she told him not to bother. "Don't waste your breath. I think we already established I know you pretty well. There's something on your mind and you might feel better talking about it."

"Probably not."

"Try me," she insisted.

There was a moment's hesitation, then he sighed and the resistance seemed to drain out of him. "I was thinking about my dad."

"Because of what Mr. Gibson said." It wasn't a question.

"Partly," he admitted. "But mostly I was remembering. He would have loved this stuff."

"So that's where you got it," she said. "Your dad had the geek gene."

"Yeah." His smile was a little sad. "He's the one who encouraged my interest in technology. If it was up to my mom, we'd be using a hammer and chisel on a rock."

She laughed. "Computer averse, is she?"

"More like dead set against." He shook his head ruefully. "She's scared of it. If anyone touches her TV remote control and starts pushing buttons, she freaks."

"Even you?"

"Especially me." His grin was wicked and fleeting. "There's hell to pay because she swears nothing works after I'm finished. She gets it just the way she wants it and everyone had better keep their mitts off or suffer the consequences. Dad would eat this up."

The words, tone and regretful expression tugged at Olivia's heart. "You still miss him, don't you?"

"Yeah." He set the tablet down.

"Family was important to him." Olivia remembered that awful day. Her parents were deeply shocked and saddened when Kevin O'Keefe, their neighbor and friend, had a sudden massive heart attack and died. It was the first time she'd seen her mother cry. "He was a good man."

Brady nodded. "When he changed jobs to stop traveling so much for work I'd just started middle school and played baseball and soccer. He came to all my games. Every one. No matter how badly we lost, he found something good about the way I played and the team as a whole."

"He was a wonderful dad. It's good he was around more so you could spend that time with him."

"Was it?"

"Of course." She was surprised that he'd question it. Time with loved ones was precious. "Why?"

"I don't know. If he'd spent less time at home, he wouldn't have been so much a part of my life. Maybe it wouldn't have been so hard when he was gone."

Olivia had never heard him talk like this. He was always the brilliant, charming, teasing, intense and hardworking founder and president of O'Keefe Technology. She'd never realized how hard he took the personal loss, how profoundly hurt he still was.

She started to say something when she heard her name. Turning, she recognized Rebecca Johnson, a local real estate broker they'd worked with to buy a piece of land for Brady's corporate offices.

There was no way to ignore the woman who joined them. "Rebecca, I would say it's a small world, but this is Blackwater Lake."

"No kidding." The attractive, fortyish blonde laughed.

"Is that why you're leaving us for sun, sand and a mysterious man?"

Dear God, here we go again, she thought. "It's a job opportunity."

The other woman tsked at Brady. "You couldn't do anything to keep her here?"

"I tried my best." He folded his arms over his chest. "She's determined."

"I guess so. You'll visit often, I hope."

"Definitely." Olivia got the feeling Rebecca had a time crunch and was glad of it.

"Good. I have to run and pick up my daughter from the library. Take care, you two."

When they were alone again, Brady grinned at her. "It's nice to know some things don't change."

"No matter how much we wish they would."

"California is big and impersonal. There's something endearing about a small town where people have a way of making everything their business. You're too stubborn to admit it, Liv, but you're going to miss it."

The only thing she would admit, and only to herself, was that she would miss him. Terribly.

"California will be an adventure," she said.

"Right."

"And before that, I'm taking some time off. A long vacation somewhere warm."

But she wondered if anywhere Brady wasn't could possibly feel warm.

Chapter Eleven

"These sketches are very impressive." Brady looked up at Alex McKnight.

The building contractor, who also happened to be his friend, had brought in some drawings for the O'Keefe Technology corporate office his architect fiancée, Ellie Hart, had done. Alex was working on a job in the area and agreed to stop by to show Brady the ideas. He was glad for the distraction. Several days had passed since he and Olivia had gone to the local electronics store, and ever since Brady had been thinking about his dad.

Alex was sitting in a chair on the other side of the desk, carefully gauging Brady's reaction. "Ellie wanted me to remind you that nothing is carved in stone yet. Walls, plumbing, anything can be moved, added or subtracted."

"Understood." Brady glanced down at the rendering of the impressive building, paved parking lot surrounded by trees and Blackwater Lake in the distance. At the street entrance there was a sign announcing O'Keefe Technology.

"This feels like a big threshold, the brink of something very important."

Brady wished his father were here to share this moment. His mother often told him that his dad was watching, that he could see his success and was proud. But that never made him feel better. It never filled up the hole in his life where his father had been. He couldn't see the pride on Kevin O'Keefe's face, couldn't hear, "Attaboy. Great job."

He still remembered a certain tone in his dad's deep, booming voice, the one he used when Brady had caught a ball against the right-field fence, or scored a soccer goal. He'd meant what he told Olivia. A part of him regretted getting so close to his father because if he hadn't, losing him wouldn't still hurt.

"A building definitely makes a statement," Alex agreed.

Brady nodded thoughtfully. "It's tangible proof that a pretty successful web hosting, web designing company is really a conglomerate. When I make news, and I will, a picture of my building will come on the screen. The viewing public will equate that structure with my company and it needs to be exciting and inspiring."

Alex grinned. "You sound like Ellie. She'd be the first to agree with you about that."

"No wonder she's so good at what she does." Brady studied the drawing. "Okay. I want to do some research—architectural stuff. It's important to get the outside right, then work on the office space."

"Absolutely. We need to incorporate the two visions for efficiency, functionality and ambience."

"I want to live with this." Brady held up the drawing. "Run it by Olivia—"

Damn. She'd be gone soon and would miss the expansion. That seemed wrong on so many levels. He couldn't imagine doing this on his own. Actually, that wasn't true. He couldn't imagine doing it without *her*.

"Something wrong, Brady? Where is Olivia?"

"At lunch." He met the other man's gaze. "I want her opinion on what you've given me."

"If you have any questions, I'll do my best to answer them. Ellie was really bummed about not being here for the meeting, but she has a doctor's appointment." Excitement, pride and something resembling fear sparked in the other man's eyes. "We're getting down to the wire. The baby's due in about four weeks."

"Wow. You don't look like you're freaking out yet."

"I am on the inside," he admitted. "And I've been through this once before. At least the birth part."

Brady knew his friend had been married before, to a woman who had lied to him about the paternity of the child she'd been carrying. Soon after the baby was born she left him for the man who'd fathered said child. That had to have been really tough.

Brady also knew his friend had grieved over the son he'd believed was his and had been alone for a long time after his wife left. Suddenly he was curious about what had made Alex decide to take another chance.

"You're a lucky man." He leaned back in his chair and looked at his friend. "Ellie is a special lady."

"That she is."

"When are you two getting married?"

"After the baby is born. Probably some time this summer."

"Any particular reason you're waiting?" Cold feet? Brady wondered. Time to make sure it wasn't a mistake?

"I asked Ellie to marry me right after she found out she was pregnant and would have done it then and there."

"And?"

"She turned me down."

Brady figured if he asked Olivia she would know all the particulars of Alex and Ellie's romance. All the women in Blackwater Lake probably knew what had gone down. He didn't have a clue and counted on his assistant to keep him in the know on local news.

"Why did she say no?" he asked his friend.

"Said she didn't want duty to be motivation for marriage. And I shouldn't feel any obligation. That she could take care of herself and the baby."

"I take it that didn't go over well with you?"

Alex grinned now, but he probably hadn't at the time. "She really ticked me off, but it gets better."

"Oh?"

"She went back to Texas without telling me. So I followed her. Of course."

"Right." He waited for more and when it wasn't forthcoming he asked, "Why?"

"At the time I told myself it was all about my child. I wasn't going to let her keep me away from him."

"Him? It's a boy?"

"Figure of speech. We don't know yet." He shrugged. "Ellie wants to be surprised, so we're waiting."

"So you chased her down because of the baby. At the time, you said. Meaning there was more to it?"

"Yeah." Alex rested his elbows on his knees. "Her folks helped me see that I loved her. She felt the same way about me, but I had to back off and let her figure that out."

"Since the two of you are engaged, I guess she did?"

"Yeah. She came back to Blackwater Lake and the third time I proposed, she said yes." Alex looked pretty pleased about that. In fact, this was the happiest he'd looked in a very long time.

"So why are you waiting to get married?"

"We decided it would be best to do it after the baby's born. She wants her family to be here. And the Harts of Texas are some high-powered businessmen. They need a little lead time, according to her." Alex shrugged. "Just between you and me, I think they'd drop everything to be here whenever their little sister gets married."

"How is she feeling?" Brady decided he needed to explain that question. "My sister had some issues toward the end of her pregnancy. She had to stay off her feet."

"I remember." His friend leaned back in his chair. "You did double duty and filled in for her a lot at the ice-cream parlor."

"Right." He could never have done that if Olivia hadn't been here to keep things running smoothly with his business.

"And everything worked out. How old is Danielle now?"

An image of his niece with chocolate ice cream all over her face popped into his mind and he couldn't help smiling. "She's a little over a year. Cute as can be."

"Spoken like a proud uncle." Alex nodded. "Makes a guy wonder why you don't have any kids yet."

The question made him think about what Maggie had said. That he was getting to that age where people were questioning why he wasn't married. If he was honest about why he wouldn't let anyone close, he'd get the talk about taking a chance.

"Because I haven't met anyone like Ellie yet."

"She is definitely one of a kind. I'm grateful every day that I found her first. She's doing fine, by the way. Thank God," he added. "Says she's big as the buildings she designs."

"Good. I'm glad all is well." He pointed at his friend. "I better get a wedding invitation."

"Top of the list, buddy." A question slid into his eyes. "I heard that Olivia is taking a job in California."

"Yeah. She gave her notice right after the first of the year, but I managed to convince her to stay until the company retreat is over."

"As I recall, that's coming up pretty soon, no?"

Brady nodded. "Two weeks."

"Good executive assistants are hard to find."

"Preaching to the choir, my friend. Fortunately Olivia found me a replacement."

"California is really different." Alex's dark eyes narrowed. "It's where I started my business, and I still have a branch of the company there. Olivia's a Blackwater Lake girl."

"I'm aware of that." He couldn't remember a time when Olivia wasn't here and didn't want to think about how it would be after she left.

"Have you tried to talk her out of it?"

"Of course." And as her departure date inched closer, he was feeling just a little north of desperate. "She's determined to go, but it's not over until it's over."

"Well, good luck with that." Alex stood. "I have to get back to the job site."

"Thanks for bringing the preliminary sketches by. I'll be in touch."

"Sounds good."

Brady walked his friend to the front door then watched Alex climb in his black truck with the McKnight Construction logo on the door. The man had gone to California and come back because Blackwater Lake was a good place to live. Wouldn't Brady be doing Olivia a favor if he saved her the inconvenience of finding all that out the hard way?

He'd been helpless when he'd lost his father. But he could do something about losing Olivia. He knew she was lying about Leonard. If he could just get her to admit it, that might be the key to getting her to stay.

The first step was kissing her again. If she kissed him back the way she did last time, he could poke holes in her story. And he was willing to kiss her again if that's what it would take to get through to her. Hell, he was more than willing. It had taken every ounce of determination he had not to kiss her good-night when he'd taken her home after dinner.

Now the clock was ticking. It was crunch time. If he was going to do this, he had to pick up the pace, and there was no time like the present.

Olivia returned from lunch and parked her car in the driveway, then got out.

Getting ready for work that morning she'd decided on jeans, then tucked them into boots lined with a fur-like material—very expensive and exceedingly warm. With snow still on the ground from a storm the day before, it had seemed like a good day to go more casual than usual, and she appreciated Brady's informal dress code. She was going to miss it. Hunching her shoulders against the frigid temperature, she walked around the car toward the front steps.

"It's about time you got back." Brady's voice startled her; she hadn't seen him on the porch. He stood there with his arms folded across his chest.

She stopped and looked at him. "Why? Is there a crisis?"

"No." He walked down to meet her. "I just like it better when you're at your desk."

"So you're a beck-and-call kind of boss."

"Something like that." There was a funny look in his eyes. This was definitely out of character and there was a significant vibe that he was up to no good.

"Why are you out here?"

"What's wrong with standing on my own front porch?" he countered.

"It's just not like you. You barely pull your nose out of the computer to eat, so standing here when it's freezing outside seems a little weird."

"Wow, let me bask in the respectful tone," he said wryly. "One man's weird could be another man's turning over a new leaf."

"This is you we're talking about, so that's not likely." The frigid air was starting to penetrate her clothes. "And if you don't get out of the cold soon, you're going to get sick."

"Being cold doesn't make you sick. Viruses do." He breathed deeply of the cold, crisp, clear air. Beside them was a gently rolling area that in summer would be lush green grass. Right now there was a thick covering of white. "It's a beautiful day."

"It's twenty-two degrees," she reminded him.

"The sky has never been so blue. The sun has never shone so bright."

"Now you're waxing poetic. This level of weird is starting to scare me."

"Liv," he said, his tone dripping with sympathy, "you have to stop and smell the roses."

"I can't. Flowers have enough sense not to come out until spring."

"It's an expression."

"Right. You're trying to tell me that all of a sudden you like being outside and one with nature."

"Something like that." There was a whole lot of wicked in his eyes that made this explanation suspect.

"Well, I'm freezing." She walked past him and climbed the first step toward the porch and front door. "Knock yourself out, nature boy."

"I'm sorry, what did you just call me?" There was laughter more than anything else in his voice.

"You heard me. I have work to do—"

And that's when something that felt a lot like a snowball hit her in the back, right near her collar so that the coldness slid down inside her sweater, leaving a wet trail. A shiver raced over her spine and escalated the spirit of revenge into he's-going-down mode.

"That was a cheap shot and completely unworthy of you." She dropped her purse by the front door and turned to face him.

"What can I say? I'm a cheap guy." Completely unrepentant, he had the audacity to grin. "But personally I think it was awesome and finally all that high-school baseball paid off."

"It was underhanded." She marched down the steps and stood a few feet away from him. "You are dead, mister."

She bent down and scooped up a handful of snow and hurled the icy projectile at him. It was infuriating when he ducked and the mass sailed by, leaving him unscathed.

Even more infuriating, he laughed. "You're going to have to do better than that."

He grabbed up some snow and threw it in her direction, hitting her in the face. She tried again and he dodged again. Now she was really getting ticked and figured the best way to nail him was getting in close. They circled each other, watching for a move, a sign of weakness. Their shoes crunched on the snow and their breath made white clouds between them.

Brady's foot slipped, but he caught himself and didn't go down. Still, it gave her an opening. She bent and took a fistful of snow and pitched it in his direction, catching him squarely in the chest.

"Lucky shot," he taunted.

"Skill and determination, my friend." She pumped her arm in triumph. "I played softball in high school and college."

"Hmm. I didn't know that."

"There's a lot you don't know about me," she said smugly. Because he'd never really noticed her.

That personal thought made her concentration slip for a second, giving him the chance to reach down and lob a ball of snow at her in one lightning-fast motion. The hit was dead-on and caught her just where the cold trickled down the neck of her sweater all the way to bare skin.

"That does it." Olivia was finished playing cat and mouse. "It's time for shock and awe."

"Bring it."

She squatted down and started grabbing snow, chucking it at him as fast as she could. He blocked it with his forearm while moving in on her, a frontal assault. Before she could get to her feet and run, he grabbed her and stuffed snow inside her jacket while she squirmed to break his hold.

Unfortunately, he had her on size, weight and strength. That just made her more determined to get her licks in wherever she could. But the snow was slippery and he lost his balance. They fell into the icy softness with Brady on top of her.

He levered some of his weight onto his forearms to keep from crushing her, but showed no inclination to move away and let her up. Their faces were very close and his breath stirred her hair.

"Are you ready to concede defeat?" he asked.

"Never give up, never surrender."

"Even though I've got you where I want you?"

If only that were true, she thought. "This was my plan all along."

He laughed and resumed shoving snow inside her jacket while she shrieked at the bitter coldness of it and struggled to get away. At the same time she was doing her darnedest to inflict some cold, wet damage on him. She managed to get some down his back and in his face, but she was tiring.

Apparently Brady was, too, because he said, "Care to talk terms of surrender yet?"

His mouth was inches from hers and she ached for him to kiss her again, but probably that wasn't the negotiating point he meant. Just like that, the fight went out of her and the cold slipped in. She shivered and her teeth started to chatter.

"That's it. Consider the white flag raised." He levered himself off her, then stood and reached down a hand, pulling her to her feet. "You need to get inside and change those wet clothes before you catch your death."

"C-cold doesn't make you sick. V-viruses do." She was trying to be sassy, but the violent shivering took the starch out of her words. "How c-come you're not freezing?"

"Who says I'm not? If you hadn't caved, I was getting ready to throw in the towel."

"You're just saying that to make me feel better."

"Is it working?"

"N-not so much. I can't feel my hands and the feet are going f-fast."

Brady hustled her up the front steps and grabbed her

purse before opening the door. "Up there," he ordered, pointing to the stairs. "Take a long, hot shower."

"Okay."

"I'll find something dry for you to wear."

Olivia nodded and concentrated on putting one foot in front of the other. She went into the guest room bath and shut the door before peeling off her wet clothes with fingers barely functioning, they were so cold. She turned on the shower and let it get good and warm before stepping inside.

As the soothing water beat down on her she breathed, "Heavenly."

She stayed that way for a long time and was beginning to wonder how big Brady's water heater was when she heard a knock.

"Liv?" The door opened.

Brady! The shower-door glass was frosted and he couldn't see anything even if he walked in, which he didn't. But her body responded as if he was staring right at her. Heat pooled low in her belly and her thighs quivered. Her breasts felt heavy and ached to be touched.

"Liv? Are you okay?"

"Fine."

"I left some sweats on the bed for you."

"Thanks," she called over the sound of the water.

"I'm going to make you a hot drink. Meet me in the kitchen when you're finished."

"Okay."

The door closed and with a sigh of regret, she turned off the shower then grabbed a towel from the bar on the wall just outside it. She wrapped the terry cloth around her hair and took a second one to dry her body. On the bed she found black sweatpants, a long-sleeved gray T-shirt and thick wool socks. She had a few hair things in the bathroom and managed to comb through the wet strands then pull them up with a scrunchy. Looking in the mirror at her flushed, makeup-free cheeks, she sighed.

"Ready or not, here I come," she said to the reflection.

In the kitchen she saw Brady pulling two mugs from the microwave. His hair was wet, too, and he'd changed into dry jeans and a T-shirt.

"This is, without a doubt, the weirdest day I've ever had at work," she said.

"I know what you mean." He was just setting the mugs on the counter.

"These pants are really big. I'm afraid they'll fall down. So this workday could possibly get even more bizarre."

Brady finally looked over and when he saw her, his eyes flashed with something hot and intense. He swallowed hard. "Call it a job perk. One of the advantages of working at home is having dry clothes available for a spontaneous snowball fight."

"Easy for you to say. They're your clothes and fit you."

"You might not believe this—" His gaze met and held her own. There was a ragged edge to his voice that was different. Exciting. "It's not that easy for me to say."

Olivia's heart skipped and she couldn't think of a single sassy or coherent response.

Brady picked up a steaming mug and moved close, holding it out to her. "Another perk of this job. It's probably safe to say that you'll never have another one where the boss makes you hot chocolate."

"It's true—"

Without warning the reality of the situation hit her. She wanted to say that where she was going in California there wouldn't be any snow and the Pacific Ocean was a perk, but she couldn't get the words past the knot of emotion lodged in her throat.

To her horror and humiliation, tears started rolling down her cheeks. She turned away and covered her face with her hands. Behind her she heard Brady swear, then he was there, his hands on her shoulders, turning her against his chest. Strong arms came around her, warming her as surely as the hot shower had done.

"Don't cry, Liv. I'm sorry. I didn't mean to make you sad. Please stop. I'm a jerk. An idiot. A moron. Everything you've ever said about me."

"I n-never called you a moron—" She laughed but the sound was more like a choked sob. It was the hardest thing she'd ever done, but she lifted her face away from his chest and looked up. "Don't feel bad. It's nothing you said. I'm just tired and emotional."

He cupped her cheek in his big, warm palm and brushed a tear away with his thumb. "You're allowed."

He was looking at her in a way that made her feel intensity rolling off him and wrapping around her. If someone snapped a video of them right this minute, she was sure it would show her body language begging for the touch of his mouth to hers.

In the next instant he kissed her and it was as if a switch flipped on. His mouth was greedy and demanding and she met him with a hunger that could no longer be ignored. Their breathing escalated, mingled, and the sound of passion was all she could hear.

And then she felt his hand move, sliding up under the big shirt, easily finding her bare breast. Finally. Finally she had his attention. He noticed her the way she'd always wanted.

Chapter Twelve

Olivia sighed as Brady cupped her breast in his wide palm. She'd waited forever to be in this moment with him and it felt better than the best day she'd ever had. His thumb brushed over her nipple, just the lightest touch, but it zapped her and sent sexy signals straight to her core.

She slid her arms up around his neck and he dropped his hands to her waist, pulling her closer, nestling her against proof that he wanted her as much as she wanted him. Standing on tiptoe in the wool socks out of his dresser, she kissed him with everything she had, everything that was in her heart.

It was a while before Brady dragged his mouth from hers and struggled to catch his breath. "You pack quite a wallop, lady, and not just throwing snow."

There was desire in his eyes, but it was laced with something that looked a lot like surprise.

He hadn't expected to want her?

So why had he kissed her? The last time it had been about challenge and restoring his reputation. Moments ago she'd thought he was caught up in the moment, just as she was. But what if it was something more underhanded? Like part of a campaign to convince her to stay.

Her best day ever just went south and she took a step back, out of his arms.

"Nice try, Brady."

"What?" His eyes narrowed as he blew out a breath, on his way to regaining control.

"You're trying to trip me up." She hoped she was wrong, but if not, he'd stooped that low, so why shouldn't she? "That was an attempt to drive a wedge between me and Leonard."

"Believe me when I tell you that just now Leonard never crossed my mind." His voice was deep, edgy, just this side of dangerous.

If only she didn't find that so darned exciting.

Olivia gripped the elastic waistband of the sweatpants she was wearing. Partly to keep them from falling off, but also to keep him from seeing that her hand was shaking. That wouldn't project the image she was going for in forcefully declaring that seducing her wouldn't work. "Okay. You didn't deserve that. But this needs to be said. Whatever crossed your mind just now isn't a good idea."

"I couldn't agree more."

"This was nothing more than a weak moment." Olivia did her best not to be disappointed that he didn't try to change her mind. "And weak moments are the best way to ruin a perfectly wonderful friendship."

"Right again." He dragged his fingers through his hair.

"So we understand each other. Good." It gave her some satisfaction that his hand was shaking, too. "I'm going to put my wet clothes in the dryer now."

"Okay."

She started out of the kitchen, leaving the mug of hot chocolate that was now cold. In the doorway she stopped and looked at him. "This has to be said, too. Just in case you're thinking that I'll have another weak moment for you to capitalize on and take something to the next level, you should know that it's not going to happen."

Without waiting for a response, she left the room, wondering if she'd become a proficient enough liar to convince him he couldn't take her to bed. Because if he ever kissed her like that again, he could take her anywhere he wanted to go.

Several days later Brady walked into his kitchen to open a bottle of wine. His gaze was drawn to the spot by the island where he'd stood with Olivia when the need to kiss her and touch her had overwhelmed his rational thought and common sense. Though she was in the other room with O'Keefe Technology's chief website designer, the same feeling overtook him.

He suddenly realized that he could never be in this room again without thinking about her, wanting her. What was he supposed to do with that information? She was determined to leave—and had flat out said that seducing her into changing her mind wouldn't work. The devil of it was when he'd kissed her, he'd had no ulterior motive. The only thing on his mind was having her; it had nothing to do with talking her into staying.

"Brady?" Olivia's voice came from behind him. "Do you need help?"

Yes, but not the way she meant.

Brady braced himself, then turned to look at her. Fortunately Ian Bradshaw was there, too.

"Why don't you get some glasses, Liv?" He looked at his friend. "Is a Jordan Cab okay with you?"

"One of my favorite wines."

Ian had come to Blackwater Lake a couple days early for the employee weekend so they could get some business out of the way before the fun started. Because Brady was breaking the news about her leaving the company, Olivia had agreed to his request to stay for this meeting. Now, for the first time ever, he had mixed feelings about her sitting in on business.

Ian Bradshaw was over six feet tall with dark hair and eyes. They'd met in college and became friends. When Brady grew his company to the point of expanding, he'd thought of his buddy to take over website design so Brady could focus on the business end of things. Olivia had once said Ian was very good-looking and could leave his shoes under her bed any time.

The comment had annoyed him and he hadn't understood why. Now he wondered if it was jealousy that had been simmering for a very long time.

"How was the weather in California?" Olivia asked.

The other man leaned back against the counter and crossed his legs at the ankles. "Cold."

"Define cold," she said wryly.

"About sixty."

"Oh, my. However do you stand it? Makes me shiver just thinking about it." She took the filled wineglass and handed it to their guest.

"What?" Ian said. "Does it really get that cold here?"

"Yes." She grinned.

"Then you'll be very happy when you leave Blackwater Lake."

"I have mixed feelings about the move," she admitted.

While he poured wine into the other two glasses, Brady

listened to them banter and decided the teasing behavior could be called flirting. Leonard would be jealous. However, if there really was a Leonard, he would challenge Brady to a duel for what had happened in this very room.

"Do you want me to put together some appetizers? It could be awhile before dinner."

"Don't go to any trouble," Ian protested.

"You always say that." Olivia smiled. "Makes me want to fuss over you."

That comment twisted Brady's gut into knots. He took a healthy sip of wine, then asked his friend, "How's Georgia?"

"We split up." Ian's mouth pulled tight and when he looked up, his expression was bleak and colder than the dead of winter in Montana. "After losing our son, the odds of our marriage surviving were against us, but we were determined to beat them." He shrugged. "We didn't."

Olivia made a sympathetic sound and touched his arm. "I'm so sorry to hear that. Are you all right?"

"Fine as I can be. Georgia, too. We just weren't fine together anymore."

"If there's anything I can do—" Brady didn't like knowing there was a problem without a solution. It was messy and complicated and why he didn't get serious or personal.

"You're keeping me busy," Ian said. "That's the best thing for me."

"Good. Let's go sit in the family room. Relax."

"You two go ahead," Olivia said. "I'll make up a few snacks. It's no trouble."

The two of them walked into the other room and sat on the leather corner group, at a right angle to each other. There were coasters on the dark wood coffee table, thanks to his ever-efficient executive assistant. Not for the first time he wondered what he'd do without her. But the feeling was becoming less about business. It was personal.

Brady made small talk with Ian and a few minutes later Olivia brought a tray of cheese, crackers, olives and marinated mushrooms along with plates, forks and cocktail napkins. Left to his own devices, he was pretty sure it would be a bag of chips and a can of peanuts. Mixed nuts, if he was feeling in a gourmet frame of mind.

"Here you go, gentlemen." She set everything out, then sat beside Brady. But far enough away so that no part of their bodies touched.

Still, he could feel the heat from her body and that was exceedingly distracting.

"Okay, guys." She looked at each of them. "It's time to entertain me with college stories. Tales of your misspent youth."

"You've heard all the good ones," Ian said. "If there were any more, neither of us would have graduated."

Brady felt a jab, because he hadn't technically graduated. He'd left before finals in his senior year. Burnout was a bitch.

"There was that art class we took," he said.

"I'd forgotten about that." Ian's grin was immediate and wicked with memories.

"Go on." Olivia looked at each of them. "What? No details? Let me help. What kind of art class? Origami? Sculpture? Water colors? History of Impressionism?"

Brady smiled at his friend and at the same time they both said, "Sketching."

"I have a feeling where this is going, but let me be the straight man." She tapped her lip. "Did you draw flowers? Landscapes? Ocean scenes?"

"The human body," Ian clarified.

"Parts? Hands, arms, feet? Noses? Mouths?" she asked sweetly.

"All of the above. At first," Brady said. "Then we put the parts together."

"The final exam was a live model." Ian's voice was full of wistful nostalgia. "Nude."

"The professor said yours had two heads," Brady reminded him.

"It was shadowing," Ian protested. "I think that was my only B in college."

Olivia tried to look stern and disapproving but couldn't hold back the laughter. "You guys are pigs."

"Oink," Ian said.

"Thank you." Brady grinned at her. He loved making her smile. It just plain made him feel good inside.

"Do you remember Henry's sketch?" Ian asked. "He drew a stick figure."

Brady's smile faded. He still missed his best friend, the one he'd followed to that particular college where they'd almost finished growing up together.

"Are you talking about Henry Milton?" Olivia looked at each of them.

"That's right." Ian's smile was melancholy around the edges. "The art class was his idea, and he was quite clear that naked girls were the reason we should take it."

Olivia nodded then looked at Brady. "He was your best friend in high school, no?"

"Yes." The loss and waste of such a brilliant mind and sparkling wit got to Brady as if it had happened yesterday.

Olivia was staring at him, but before she could say anything, Ian's cell phone rang. He took it from the case hooked on his belt and looked at the ID. "Sorry. I have to take this. It's from my assistant. Could be awhile."

"You can go in the office," Olivia said. "It's quiet in

there." Olivia put her hand on Brady's arm as Ian walked out of the room. "What's wrong? And before you say nothing, you should know I'm not letting you blow me off. It's about Henry. You were fine until Ian mentioned him. Wasn't he killed in a car accident?"

"Yeah. Our last semester of college. We were rear-ended and the guy was going so fast we were pushed into a tree. Henry died instantly."

"And you weren't hurt," she guessed.

"Bumps and bruises." He shook his head. "It wasn't that long after my dad died."

"I knew about the accident but didn't put it together that it was so soon after losing your father. The loss still affects you deeply." Statement, not question.

Brady nodded. "One minute Henry was alive and we were full of plans for the future. The next he was gone." He looked at her, the sympathy swirling in her eyes nearly shattered him. "He was like the brother I never had. When we weren't in art class, we were working on computer technology. After graduation we planned to start the business together."

"Is that why you didn't take finals?" she asked. "Because Henry couldn't?"

"I don't know." But probably.

"And sometimes your accomplishments feel disloyal?" she asked.

"He never had a chance to see our plans come to be."

She nodded thoughtfully. "Here's the thing…I could tell you to stop it, but I know you and that's not the way you roll. So, think about it this way. Your friend is still here."

"Come on, Liv—"

"Seriously," she protested. "If not for knowing him, you wouldn't be the man you are. The *businessman* you are. Henry is in every product you've developed, every client signed on, every new app. Every time the business grows it's because of ideas the two of you brainstormed together. Even the new corporate offices will have a part of him."

"Maybe a plaque in the lobby with his name on it. A public dedication."

"Great idea," she said. "If you could change what happened, you would. If you could bring him back, you would. No one doubts that, but it's not possible. All you can do is make sure he continues to live in hearts and memories."

It was weird, Brady thought, the sensation that a weight had just lifted from his chest. As if she'd given him absolution. He dragged air into his lungs.

"Thank you, Liv. I never thought about it like that." He drew her into his arms. *Just a hug,* he told himself. But the fresh, pure scent of her skin, her hair, made him crave more.

He pulled back a little, but didn't let her go. Staring at the tempting curve of her mouth, he recognized the irresistible feeling coming over him again. Kissing her was something he wanted so much his chest ached from it and he started to lower his mouth to hers.

"Okay. If anything changes call me back." Ian was just outside the room.

Olivia slid away from him and folded her hands in her lap, the image of a good schoolgirl who'd almost been caught doing something wicked and wild. She could try and say this temptation was about trying to get her to stay, but that wasn't it at all.

This wasn't about O'Keefe Technology. It had nothing to do with the fact that the clock was ticking and she'd be gone soon. What he felt was far more simple and basic than that. Kissing her had tapped into his lust and he couldn't forget about it, no matter how hard he tried. He *wanted* her.

And as she'd told him more than once, he always got what he wanted.

It was Friday night and the O'Keefe Technology employee-appreciation-weekend cocktail-party kickoff was getting started. Olivia's feelings were conflicted on every level. Relief that the big shindig was finally here. Sadness because it was finally here and she'd be leaving soon. Then there was her personal confusion about the mixed signals Brady had been sending her.

Since she'd given her notice, he'd kissed her twice, the best kisses she'd ever had. In between he'd taken her out for a romantic dinner that ended with a brotherly buss on the cheek. What was that about?

Then, a few days ago, she'd realized how deeply Brady was still affected by the deaths of his father and best friend. It didn't take a talented shrink to realize he kept a distance from people. No one was going to get past his defenses and put him in a position to be hurt again.

Right now she didn't have time to think about the fall-out from that revelation. She was sitting at a table in the lobby of the Blackwater Lake Lodge to check in employees and hand out name tags along with a list of activities for the following day. So far she'd been too busy to appreciate the Lodge's gorgeous stone fireplace that rose to the second floor. There was a cozy couch and club chairs in front of it where people sat and chatted. Area rugs in earth-tone colors covered the wood floor and the registration desk was behind the table set up for her to cross off names as employees came in.

Two men and a woman stopped in front of her and she recognized them from the Los Angeles area office. She smiled brightly and said, "Tony Shay, George Collier and Carrie Atkins. Welcome."

The blonde woman in her early twenties looked impressed. "Olivia! It's great to see you again. Thanks for remembering us. You have a good memory."

"It's a gift." She heard footsteps just before Brady stopped beside her table.

She looked up and her breath caught. That happened sometimes when it completely sneaked up on her how handsome he was. Tonight he was wearing tan slacks and a navy blazer with gold buttons. Dress code was casual for everyone, but he'd upped his game tonight and she had the thready pulse and heart flutters to prove it.

"What are you doing here?" she asked.

"It's my party."

"I mean here at check-in," she amended.

"Just wanted to help you greet my employees."

"Okay, then. Have you guys met our boss, Brady O'Keefe?"

She held out her hand to indicate the three who'd just arrived and she made introductions.

Tony looked impossibly geeky. Straight brown hair, dark eyes and square-framed black glasses could do that to a computer guy. "On her last trip to Los Angeles, Olivia mentioned that there were changes coming to the company. Should we be concerned about downsizing? Layoffs?"

"Absolutely not," Brady said. "We have expansion plans for the near future. I need to hire more ambitious, smart young people like the three of you."

"That's a relief." George looked like a surfer with his sun-bleached blond hair and blue eyes. "I was thinking about buying a house."

"You might want to wait on that until after tomorrow night's announcement," Brady said.

"Why don't you tell us now?" Carrie coaxed.

"My lips are sealed until dinner tomorrow. And speaking of secrecy—" There was a look in his eyes and Olivia knew she wouldn't like what he was going to say. "When you saw Olivia on her last trip to L.A., did she mention a man? Someone special?"

The three of them looked at each other with blank expressions. Carrie was their spokeswoman. "I don't recall her talking about anyone outside of work."

"Really? Hmm." His tone was skeptical. "No one named Leonard?"

"What's the last name?" Tony asked.

"I can give you the middle name, too." He met her gaze and there was laughter in his eyes. "Leonard Sebastian Honeycut."

"Doesn't ring a bell," Carrie said, giving Olivia a what-are-you-thinking look before blanking her expression. "You guys?"

"Nope," Tony said. "Never heard of him."

"Me, either," George echoed.

"So she never talked about meeting someone outside the office?" Brady persisted.

"Not to me." Carrie looked at her colleagues, who shook their heads. "We did go out for drinks and dinner a couple of times. Thank you for that, by the way."

"You're welcome. Happy employees are productive employees."

"We like working for you, for this company." Carrie met Olivia's gaze and it was clear the young woman had made up her mind which side her bread was buttered on. "As far as I know, there's no one named Leonard on the payroll."

"Brady, stop interrogating them," Olivia scolded.

It wasn't like him to do that. She got the feeling he was up to something.

"I'm just making small talk," he defended, then looked at his three young employees. "But she's right. You go in and have fun."

"Thanks, Mr. O'Keefe."

"It's Brady." He smiled his charming smile, the one that won over men and women, friends and enemies alike. "Enjoy yourselves. You've earned it. I appreciate your loyalty and hard work."

"Yes, sir."

The employees walked away and Olivia was alone with him. This was as good a time as any to give him a piece of her mind.

"That was completely unprofessional."

"What?"

"Asking about Leonard." She glared at him. "This is business. You're the president of this company, not the gossip columnist for a Hollywood rag sheet. You set the tone."

"I am the president and as such I should get to ask anything I want."

"Not about my personal life."

"Speaking of that," he said, completely unrepentant, "it seems that no one knows anything about Leonard. It's as if he's a ghost."

Kind of, but she wasn't prepared to confirm it. "And that remark is exactly what I mean. You put those poor kids on the spot just now."

"Not really. I was asking about events in a remote office of my company. That's what this weekend is all about. Connecting with my employees."

"Not when you're connecting about my social life," she argued.

"This is a social occasion,"

"But still under the heading of business. It's a professional setting and Leonard is personal." Brady had no idea how personal, and she planned to keep it that way. She stood up but he still towered over her. "It's not the right place to quiz them about the personal stuff. Which I keep separate—whether I'm here or somewhere else traveling for the company."

Brady took a step closer and their bodies were inches apart. Suddenly heat sparked in his eyes. "What's wrong with mixing business and pleasure?"

A thrill shimmied down her spine, darn it. She was almost home free and needed to be strong. "It's never a good idea. And I'm sure you're aware of that. Probably in the first chapter of the textbook for college business class one-oh-one it lists all the negative aspects of doing that."

It was awfully tempting to call his bluff, though. He'd been baiting her for a couple of weeks now and if she believed taking him up on the challenge would change anything, she'd do it in a heartbeat. But she wanted a family. She needed someone to love her, someone she could fall in love with. He'd shut that part of himself down for so long, it was just possible that no one could turn it back on.

"Here's the thing, Liv. Kisses don't lie." When she opened her mouth to protest, he touched a fingertip to her lips, trapping the words in her throat. "We can debate the hows of it happening until hell won't have it, but that's not important."

"Really?"

"Yes. What's important is that you kissed me back. You know it and I know it. The reality is that if you were happy with Leonard, you'd have shut it down before I had a chance to *know* you were kissing me back."

Defending her make-believe boyfriend was the only

comeback she could muster. Confirming she *had* kissed him back was a dangerous place to go. "That's not fair to Leonard."

"Let's get something straight, Olivia. I care about you, not Leonard. And if I can take you to bed, he's clearly not the man for you. That's information you need to have before giving up everything for him." There was a fierce possessive determination in his eyes before he turned and walked away.

Olivia was pretty sure that Brady O'Keefe had just given her fair warning that he planned to seduce her.

Chapter Thirteen

And if I can take you to bed...

Olivia was pretty sure there was no *if* about it.

The thought had been rolling around in her head for twenty-four hours. It was Saturday night and she was sitting beside Brady at the employee dinner. She hadn't seen him all day, since they'd both been busy sitting in on different workshops and networking with employees from the various regions. Mostly she'd been working hard at avoiding him.

There was no way to duck him now. She'd made the seating arrangements for this dinner in advance and they were side by side at the head table with Ian Bradshaw and Jake Barnes, vice president in charge of company research and development.

"The restaurant looks great." Brady leaned closer and his breath stirred her hair.

Normally tables filled the center of the room, but tonight they were arranged so that a space was empty for dancing after dinner.

She looked at him. "The manager was fantastic about working with me. But I guess when you can afford to reserve the place for a private party, it buys you a whole lot of cooperation."

"You had them move all the tables."

"Yes." Theirs was right in front of the fireplace, where flames snapped and crackled cheerfully.

Salads had been eaten and removed. Now the waitstaff was serving dinner to the employees first. While they waited, Brady poured her another glass of red wine. She was feeling the first one a little and realized between being super busy and really keyed up, she hadn't eaten much that day.

She looked at Brady, trying to read his mind. "Are you trying to get me drunk?"

"What if I am?"

"Bad idea. I have to drive home."

His eyes widened in surprise. "You don't have a room here at the lodge?"

"No. I live local."

"Me, too, but I have a room. Suite, actually. This is supposed to be fun and relaxing. Blow off steam. Relieve a little stress."

To not have a room under the same roof with him would be less stressful. "I decided I'd rather sleep in my own bed."

"We'll see about that."

When the corners of his mouth curved into a smile, her heart started to pound. She wasn't sure if the words made her hopeful or scandalized. She'd been prepared for his usual tactics to change her mind about resigning. She'd braced for offers of a generous raise. Promotion.

Delays in hiring her replacement. She'd even made up a fake boyfriend to create a safe zone. But now she was in uncharted territory, because she'd never stood her ground and actually made it this far in the resignation process.

After what he'd said last night, she knew Leonard's usefulness was pretty much over, because Brady was right. If he could make her kiss him back, and he had, then she had no business being with another man. He was giving her his undivided attention. How could she protect herself against what she'd wanted for almost as long as she remembered?

She didn't know what to say and decided it would be a good idea to change the subject. Fortunately the waiter put plates of food in front of them.

"So," she said, "everyone seems to be having a good time."

Brady glanced around the room where all the tables were filled with men and women laughing and talking, eating and drinking. On the boss's dime, and a very good investment of money.

His gaze swung back to her, then lowered to her cleavage. A hungry look that had nothing to do with the expensive steak on his plate slid into his eyes. "I like your dress."

"Thanks."

She didn't tell him it was new or that she'd bought it wondering if he'd notice that the black-and-silver skirt swirled in a flirty, floaty way at her knees. Or that the sleeveless straps gave way to a dangerously low neckline. It made her feel feminine and just a little wicked. Also it was a little about *how do you like me now that I'm leaving?*

"Have I seen it before?"

The words rubbed against already raw nerves and she wanted to babble, but forced herself not to. She only said, "No."

Then she picked up her fork and knife. Keeping her mouth full seemed like a good plan. She'd been taught not to talk with her mouth full.

After that the men at the table carried the conversation during dinner. Since she had a knot in her stomach the size of Montana, Olivia mostly moved the food around her plate. Before anyone noticed, the waitress removed everything and commenced dessert service. With the boss's permission to do whatever she wanted, Olivia had picked the menu, particularly the scrumptious seven-layer chocolate cake that was her favorite. How sad was it that she couldn't eat a bite of it?

Fortunately this was the part of the program where Brady would say a few words to his employees. The jury was still out on whether or not his standing up to do that would help her nerves, but she'd take what she could get.

At his signal, one of the waitstaff handed him a portable microphone. Brady tapped it to make sure the thing was on, then said, "Good evening. I hope you all enjoyed the day and this wonderful dinner."

Cheers, whistles and applause filled the room and he smiled. "Excellent. Now that you're all in a good mood, I have an announcement to make."

Everyone got eerily quiet and Olivia could see worry creep into their expressions. The three L.A. people, Tony, George and Carrie, looked at her for reassurance and she smiled. It would be all right. Brady would make it all right. But for several years the economic climate had been dismal and once you survived something like that, job insecurity was always on your mind.

"This is good news. I promise." Brady saw the uncertainty, too. "In the spring, O'Keefe Technology is breaking ground on a corporate headquarters right here in Blackwater Lake."

Olivia had known this was coming, but not what Brady would say about it publicly. The words didn't seem to reassure anyone. No doubt they were all still wondering how this change was going to affect them personally.

"First of all, you need to know that your jobs are safe. Every last one of you is part of making this company successful and I couldn't have done it without your hard work. But the time has come for aggressive expansion, and that means I need a grown-up office that's not in my house." Laughter and applause greeted his words, showing everyone was starting to relax.

"Obviously some departments will be moving here to Montana. For anyone who relocates, there will be financial help from the company. So I hope you had an opportunity to get out today and see what the beautiful town of Blackwater Lake has to offer. Scenery to take your breath away. Clean air. Summer and winter activities." He looked down at her. "Olivia and I grew up here. We can tell you from firsthand experience that it's a great place to raise a family."

She knew this was a positive thing for his company and was happy about that. But the announcement made her heart heavy. Brady was a generous and caring boss who would take care of the people who worked for him. She'd probably never have a better employer. But it also made her sad that he could think about their families even when he wouldn't take that step for himself.

"In the coming weeks, information on all of this will be forthcoming. If there are any questions, you can check with your supervisor or manager or shoot me an email. We'll try to get answers for you. With your help, we'll make this a smooth transition. Thanks again for all you do." There was more enthusiastic clapping and he waited for it to die out. "The rest of the night is for you to have fun. The DJ is set up. He'll take your musical requests and the floor is open for dancing. Have a wonderful evening. And thanks for coming to Blackwater Lake."

After his remarks, Brady handed the microphone back to someone from the restaurant staff, then he sat back down beside Olivia. The DJ started the music with a slow song.

Brady held out his hand. "We can't leave until all our guests are gone, so you might as well dance with me."

"There are the words to make a woman go warm and gooey." Apparently the knot in her stomach made her go from spineless to defiant, because she shook her head. "I don't think that's a very good idea, Brady. There are details that need attention."

Before he could challenge her, she stood and moved away. After dodging him for a while, she danced with Ian Bradshaw and Jake Barnes. Both of them were single and good-looking, but neither gave her the zing that warmed her blood or made her heart beat faster.

Several hours later Olivia was tired. The DJ had announced last call, then packed up a little after midnight. She was so ready to go home, but stragglers stood around talking for another half hour.

Brady said good-night to a group he'd been chatting up, then returned to where she was sitting by the fire. "Do you think it would be rude to ask them to leave?"

"Yeah," she said, "I'm pretty sure it would." Maybe even a little ruder than turning him down for a dance.

"Then I guess we have no choice but to wait it out."

"You can leave." Olivia wished he would. "I'll stay and supervise."

"Nope. If you're staying I am, too."

So they did. For another fifteen minutes they made small talk about the dinner while trying not to look eager for everyone to call it an evening. Finally the last four waved a good-night and shouted a "thank you for everything" while heading out the door.

Jenel Parks, the pretty blonde restaurant manager, came over. "That's a bunch of party animals who work for you, Brady."

"I prefer to think of them as enthusiastic."

"Whatever." She stifled a yawn. "I'll lock up now."

"Okay." Olivia picked up her purse and black coat. "Thanks for everything, Jenel."

"You're welcome. I look forward to next year."

Olivia felt the stab of those words, because she wouldn't be part of it. That event would be coordinated by someone else. She and Brady left the restaurant and walked down the carpeted hall toward the Lodge's lobby. Just before turning the corner, he took her hand to stop her.

"I've been waiting all night to do this."

Sexual intensity sizzled in his eyes as he cupped her face in his hands. Softly, sweetly, he touched his mouth to hers. He kissed her over and over, gently nibbling her lips and shattering her defenses at the same time.

It was awhile before he lifted his head and looked at her, passion humming through him. She tried to step away, but he wouldn't let her go.

"Time is running out, Liv. You agreed to stay through this event and now it's over. You'll be gone soon." He dragged in a deep breath. "I have enough regrets in my life and many of them I couldn't do anything about. But I don't have to live with the regret of not having you in my arms for one night."

Olivia could feel her weak protest disintegrate as soon as the echo of his words died away. She'd been right earlier. There was no way to prepare herself to walk away from this, and she couldn't do it.

She met his gaze. "So I guess you were right about me not sleeping in my own bed."

His only response was sexy smile that simmered straight through to her soul.

The elevator ride to Brady's suite was the longest and shortest of Olivia's life. She was both nervous and could hardly wait. It was a tie as to whether the upward movement or a severe case of anxiety was causing her stomach to roll. Then he linked his fingers with hers and relief trickled through her that keeping the physical connection was important to him, too. He met her gaze as he brought their joined fingers to his mouth and kissed the back of her hand.

The gesture was sweet yet erotic and made her shiver with anticipation. Her tingles had tingles; her goose bumps had goose bumps. And then they stopped at the top floor, his floor.

He let her precede him out of the elevator and guided her, settling his hand at the small of her back just where her dress stopped and bare skin began. At the end of the hall, they paused in front of a door and he took out his wallet to retrieve the key card.

"Do you have condoms in there?" She blinked up at him as the horror of her words sank in. "I have no idea why I said that."

"Don't you?" Instead of being offended, Brady seemed amused. His grin widened before he said, "It's because you're organized and leave nothing to chance."

"Is that a polite way of saying I'm a control freak?"

"Not at all." He kissed her lightly on the mouth. "But Liv?"

"What?"

"Trust me. I think ahead, too. Just relax."

Yeah, that would happen. "Okay, then."

It's just that she wanted this to be perfect. Life rarely lived up to imagination, and hers had been traveling at warp speed since he'd first kissed her.

Brady unlocked the door, then opened it and she walked in. Behind her he flipped a switch and the interior lit up. She looked around, charmed by everything she saw. There was a living room and dining area furnished in dark wood and a beautiful floral-print sofa with a chair and ottoman covered in a deep, rich hunter-green. Lamps had brass bases with scalloped cream-colored shades. There was a wet bar on the wall by the doorway that led to the bedroom.

He took her purse and set it on the table just inside the door before hanging up her coat in the closet. "Would you like a brandy? Since you won't be driving. Or sleeping in your own bed tonight."

Oh, boy. He really did think ahead. Afterward she wouldn't have to wonder whether to stay or go.

"I'd love a brandy."

"Coming right up."

He moved farther into the room, removing his suit coat and carelessly dropping it on the chair. With several quick flicks of his wrist, he loosened his tie and dragged it over his head, tossing it on top of the coat.

"Do you mind if I look around?"

"Of course not."

While he selected the correct glasses and opened the bottle, Olivia peeked in the bedroom. It was big and beautiful, a thick comforter on the bed and what seemed like a bazillion throw pillows in all shapes and sizes artfully arranged on top. The bathroom was rock and marble and glass, with a flat-screen TV and a magnifying makeup mirror, both on swing-out arms at opposite ends of the vanity.

She wandered over to French doors that opened onto a patio with a spectacular view of the mountains. From here she could see the Blackwater Lake ski resort, with bright lights to illuminate the snow. It was irresistible and she opened the doors, then walked outside. She simply couldn't believe that Brady O'Keefe had finally noticed her, that she was here and both of them knew what was going to happen. This was a pinch-yourself moment.

For a few seconds she didn't feel the cold. Then it hit her, but Brady was there, so close the heat from his body warmed her. She turned and he handed her a snifter with a small amount of amber liquid splashed in the bottom.

"What should we drink to?" His voice was deep and velvety with seduction.

One thing after another skipped through her mind, but not one seemed right. "Too much pressure. You decide."

"Okay." He thought for a moment, then said, "To you."

"And you." She touched her glass to his.

Olivia sipped and swallowed, letting the liquor burn down her throat. It settled in her stomach and warmed her from the inside out, giving everything a sort of magical glow.

When she finished her drink, Brady took the snifter from her and set both of them on the patio's table for two. Then he moved close and stared into her eyes.

"I don't think I've ever seen you look more beautiful than you do now, in the moonlight, with the Montana mountains behind you…." He stopped, seeming at a loss for words. "Simply stunning."

Her heart pounded and the moment seemed surreal. "I don't know what to say to that."

"Good. Because talking is the last thing I want to do."

He settled his hands on her hips and tugged her close before lowering his head to touch his mouth softly to hers. Her pulse went from zero to sixty in a heartbeat. Their breath mingled and escalated, making white clouds in the cold air.

When she shivered he pulled away and swore. "I'm an idiot. Let's get you back inside."

Olivia didn't feel cold, just warm, fuzzy and turned on. He could take her anywhere as long as he kissed her that way again. Sliding his arm around her waist, Brady walked her back into the suite and closed the French doors behind them.

"Now, where were we?" Indirect light from the living room illuminated the bed and she could see the sexy, amused look in his eyes.

"I think—here." She stood on tiptoe and brushed his lips with hers.

His arms came around her, pressing her soft breasts against the solid strength of his chest. He groaned and his breathing grew labored as his fingers grazed the bare skin on her back.

The next thing she knew the zipper on her dress was going down. Air whispered against her spine and she knew when she moved away, her flirty little dress would fall at her feet. Since she wasn't wearing a bra, that meant she would be naked except for panties and four-inch pumps.

Breathing hard, she pulled her mouth from his and let her arms slide down his chest. Then, taking a deep breath and a step back, she watched his expression go from intense to awe to unmistakable male approval.

"Liv, I—" He stopped and cleared his throat. "I take it back. You look more beautiful now than you did in the moonlight."

This time she knew what to say. "I'm glad you think so."

"I do."

He pulled the bottom of his dress shirt from the waist of his slacks and yanked it over his head without undoing the buttons. She started toward him and he said, "Hold that thought."

Turning away, he moved to the bed and tossed off the pillows, then dragged down the comforter, blanket and top sheet in one sweeping motion. He opened the nightstand drawer and removed a small square packet.

"You are prepared," she said.

"A regular Boy Scout."

"What if I said no?"

"I'd have been very disappointed."

The thing was, he'd all but said this was what he had in mind, so it really wasn't a surprise that he was ready. So was she.

He smiled and held out his hand. "Come here."

After stepping out of her heels, she moved closer and put her fingers in his palm, letting him tug her to him. He lifted her into his arms and set her in the center of the huge bed. Never letting his gaze drift from hers, he un-buckled his belt, unzipped his slacks, toed off his loaf-ers and removed boxers and pants, followed by his socks.

When he joined her on the soft mattress he was naked and with a sweep of his hand, her panties joined his clothes on the floor. He rolled toward her and gathered her close, threading his fingers into her hair as their mouths recon-nected. While he kissed her senseless, his palm stroked over the curve of her waist to caress her hip.

Olivia could hardly breathe. Brady took her to a place she'd never been before, where passion and desire grew until she could hardly stand it. She explored his bare chest, her palm wandering over the muscled contour while the masculine dusting of hair tickled her fingers. When she grazed his nipple, he sucked in air.

"Oh, God…" His voice was a ragged whisper. "I want you, Liv."

"Yes…" She dragged the single word out until it became a hiss.

Brady didn't hesitate. He rolled away from her long enough to grab the condom, then opened the packet and covered himself faster than seemed humanly possible. Settling himself over her, he took most of his weight on his forearms, entering her slowly, gently nudging, letting her grow accustomed to him. Eagerly she arched her hips up to meet him.

He kissed her then trailed his mouth over her chin and neck, nibbling her collarbone until finding her breast. He raked his tongue over the sensitized peak and the electric sensation started a trembling in her core that radiated outward. The instantaneous and unexpected release shattered her into a thousand pieces but he threaded his fingers with hers, squeezing gently and holding her until she was whole again.

Then he began to move and she met each thrust, ready and willing to go with him. His breathing was harsh and shallow before he suddenly went still and groaned as he buried his face in her neck. She held him and felt the corded muscles in his back as she kissed the broad curve of his shoulder, showing him with everything she had just how deep her feelings went.

It seemed like forever but was probably just moments before he lifted his head and looked into her eyes. Smiling he said, "Wow."

"That goes double for me."

He laughed and kissed the tip of her nose. "Don't go anywhere. I'll be right back."

Olivia had no intention of ever moving, except maybe to burrow more deeply into the thick mattress and pull the cozy bedding up over her body. So this was what contentment felt like. For once in her life, reality was way better than her fantasies.

Then Brady came back and slid into bed beside her, snuggling her against him. "How are you?"

"Never been better."

"I'm glad to hear that. Me, too." He kissed the top of her head, then rested his cheek to the spot his lips had just brushed. "You know this means that you can't be with Leonard."

She went completely still. Oddly enough, her make-believe boyfriend had not once crossed her mind since Brady had said he planned to take her to bed. The reality was that she'd lied to him and it was time to come clean.

Olivia took a deep breath and said, "About Leonard…"

Chapter Fourteen

Ever since Olivia had told her fake-boyfriend whopper, she'd had many opportunities to regret it, but never more than now. Confessing her transgression wasn't the sort of postsex pillow talk she'd fantasized about. She wanted to snuggle in closer, except that seemed wrong somehow, so she shied away a little but couldn't completely give up the lovely, warm circle of Brady's arms.

"Liv?" he prompted.

"Okay. I was just—" Procrastinating, mostly. She sneaked a peek at his expression, which fell under the heading Amused Indulgence. "I'm just trying to figure out how to say this."

"Just spit it out," he suggested. "How bad can it be?"

"Pretty bad." She pulled the sheet up more snugly, almost to her neck. "You have no idea how awful this is. You think I'm such a goody two-shoes. Honest and trustworthy. I just really hate to shatter your image of me."

"Liv, just say it. Seriously, you're not capable of anything that requires this much qualification."

"Okay. Spit it out." Probably for the best. "I lied. There is no Leonard Sebastian Honeycut."

His lips twitched as if he was trying to hold back laughter. "Really?"

"Yes. I know it was wrong, but the words just came out of my mouth."

"Why?"

Olivia thought back to that January day and why she'd made up her mind to quit. The alternative was that she'd turn into a dried-up old prune who wore an ancient ratty sweater. A spinster with no man, no kids, just a bunch of cats. Not that she didn't like animals, but she didn't want to be the cliché. It was the third time she'd tried to quit and she'd been determined to be successful. And then she'd said her piece and he was so cocky and cavalier.

"Do you remember when I told you I was quitting?"

His brows drew together in thought. "Vaguely."

"Let me recap." She gathered her thoughts. "First you made my decision to leave all about you. I believe the word you used was *abandon*."

"Did I?"

"Yes."

"Hmm."

He removed his arm and propped the pillows against the headboard before sitting up to settle against them. The sheet pooled at his waist, highlighting the wide chest and muscular arms. The sight was almost as intoxicating as the rogue dimple that always distracted her.

"When that didn't talk me out of it, you implied it was a new year's resolution. Same-time-next-year sort of thing. You suggested that it was my way of asking for a raise." She met his amused gaze, trying to decide if she was annoyed or still explaining why she'd lied. "Does any of this sound familiar to you?"

"A little."

"FYI, about the raise…if I wanted one, I'd ask for it."

"Understood." He folded his arms over his chest. "Please go on."

"When none of that was successful in getting what you wanted, you simply refused to accept my resignation."

"And you said you wouldn't show up. You reprimanded me for not looking for your replacement on the double."

"Wow."

"What?"

She rose up on her elbow and rested her cheek in her hand, staring at him. "Color me impressed that you were paying attention."

"I always listen to you."

"Right. Do you remember what happened after that?"

"It's a little hazy," he admitted.

"You begged."

His mouth curved up. "That's a little harsh."

"But true."

"Are we getting close to the part where you made up your mind to fib?"

"Yes." She sighed. "When none of your tactics had the desired results, you attacked and asked why I was doing this now. You said nothing had changed in my life."

He frowned. "I don't remember that."

"Of course you don't. But I do." She would always remember the humiliation and hopelessness of her pathetic life and how that fueled her determination to reinvent herself. "You were smug and so confident that my life revolved around you. That I'd always be around, at your beck and call."

"When you've got the best, the smart play is to maintain."

"I'm flattered, but twice before I tried to quit and always gave in. It would have happened again if I had nothing to fight back with. So—" she lifted a shoulder "—before I thought it through, the words came out of my mouth that I'd met a man and was moving away from Blackwater Lake."

"What about the job offer in California?"

"That's real. And it's a great opportunity." Although the fact that they were having this conversation in bed might mean everything had changed. A seed of hope started to grow. "I'm sorry, Brady. I didn't plan to lie to you, but it seemed like a good idea at the time."

He nodded. "I understand."

"You do?" She piled her pillows up and slid to a sitting position beside him. Their shoulders brushed, sending sparks of heat skipping over her skin.

"Yes. And I have a confession to make, too."

"Okay." This could be good or bad. She held her breath and waited.

"I knew you were lying."

She blinked at him for several moments then asked, "You knew? From the beginning?"

"No."

She thought she'd pulled it off rather well and admitted to a bit of satisfaction at shaking up his unshakeable confidence. Still, he didn't seem particularly upset about being lied to. "When you snooped in my email? Did you know then?"

"No."

"Did Maggie tell you?" she demanded.

"Not at first. But I figured it out."

"How?"

"Just little things. The fact that you hadn't told your mother. When I kissed you, you kissed me back. I know you better than you think. If you were in a committed relationship, you wouldn't kiss another man as if you meant it. Your story worked for a little while. But you need to face the fact that you're really not a very good liar."

Olivia started thinking back, trying to pinpoint the change. That day she'd come back from lunch. She aimed an accusing finger at him. "You were testing me. That day you were waiting for me and started the snowball fight. I thought you were acting weird."

"Really?" He grinned.

"Yes. Now that I think about it, your behavior was different even before that. When you invited me to dinner and said I should dress up. That was out of character."

"It was a romantic gesture."

"And the very first one I'd ever experienced from you." She'd been too wary to relax, but— "I had a good time that night."

Now, here they were, getting everything out in the open. *Naked,* she thought, as little bubbles of happiness floated inside her. Then she noticed his expression.

He looked uneasy. "Liv, why did you feel as if you had to resort to a make-believe boyfriend in order to convince me you were serious about quitting? Why was it that important for you to get away from me?"

That was the question. Her motivation was, no pun intended, at the heart of the matter. He didn't want anyone to get close and she wanted closeness and everything that came with it. Should she sugarcoat this and let him off the hook?

Olivia couldn't believe she was thinking like that, still protecting him. The time had come to face up to the truth and she owed him that.

"Do you remember that night I came by the house un-expectedly? It was a couple of years ago," she added.

There was a dark intensity in his eyes when he nodded. "You ended up falling asleep on my couch. Without tell-ing me what was on your mind. Although it was obvious that you had something to tell me."

"I still do. Nothing has changed."

"Once you say something, you can't take it back. Maybe it's better left unsaid." Now he didn't look cocky and confident.

"No, the truth is best." She took a deep breath, then met his gaze. "I love you, Brady. I have since I was fif-teen years old. I thought I'd outgrow the crush, but that's not what happened. Working for you only made me more sure that I'm in love with you."

Olivia stared at him, waiting for him to respond to her heartfelt declaration. The longer she waited, the more her hope began to fail until finally it was gasping for survival. He just blinked at her.

"That's what I thought."

Tears burned her eyes but she refused to let them fall. At least she could get out of this with her dignity, if not her heart, intact.

Without a word, she slid out of bed, grateful there were no lights on in the bedroom as she gathered up her clothes. She fled to the suite's living room to dress, then collected her coat and purse before letting herself out.

Brady still hadn't said a word or tried to stop her, the complete opposite of his behavior when she'd quit her job. Who knew that instead of making up a fake boyfriend, all she had to do was confess her love to get him to accept her resignation? She'd bared herself, body and soul, and his silence was answer enough.

He didn't feel the same.

And so her fantasy was really and truly over, with a completely different outcome from the one her imagination had cooked up. Real life was cruel that way, spoiling the happy ending. It had been a lot more magical in her head. She should have known when he'd poured the brandy and his toast had been "to you" and not "to us."

"There is no us and never will be."

Tears she'd kept him from seeing rolled down her cheeks as she walked away.

When Olivia didn't show up for work by ten o'clock on Monday morning, Brady started to worry. He'd known the clock was ticking on her departure after employee-appreciation weekend, but they'd agreed she would work one more week with her replacement. It wasn't like her. If he wore a watch, he could set it by her. On top of that, her replacement had arrived, but there was no one there to fine-tune her training. He'd sent the woman home with orders to read company handbooks and policy manuals again. He was too preoccupied to deal with someone who was practically a stranger.

The first hour he'd assumed Olivia was just late, even though it was out of character. Then another sixty minutes passed and he decided she was punishing him. For the record, he didn't see that he'd done anything wrong.

So during the last two hours he'd answered the phone but couldn't help anyone who'd called, because Olivia always did that. In between, he couldn't do his own work because it was impossible to concentrate, so he paced like a caged tiger between his office and her empty one.

While pacing, he had a lot of time to think and his thoughts went back to what had happened Saturday night. They'd had sex. Somehow it felt deeper and more profound than just the physical act. It was fantastic. Then she'd said she loved him and he didn't respond. Now he allowed that might have been thoughtless.

And he'd taken thoughtless to a whole new level by not contacting her. He hadn't talked to her since she'd left the Lodge, figuring that would give her some space to cool off. Again, hindsight was twenty-twenty, and he realized that might have been a mistake. To cool off presupposed that someone was angry, and maybe that's not what she was.

That left hurt. But she was very important to him and hurting her was the last thing he'd ever do. At least not on purpose. So he had to correct his thoughtless mistake and talk to her.

He took his cell phone from the case on his belt and hit speed dial. Hers was the first number and it rang several times before he got her voice mail.

"This is Olivia Lawson. Please leave your name, number and a brief message and I'll get back to you as soon as I can."

When he heard the beep Brady said, "Liv, it's me. You've got my number. Call me back."

He clicked off and his frustration built to the breaking point. Brief message, his ass. "You're late for work" was short. Ditto for saying her behavior was childish. Throwing his phone against the wall seemed like a good thing to do, but rational thought came through just in time. It was just that hearing her voice made him long for her to walk through the door, say good-morning, then sit at her desk so they could get back to normal.

And then his imagination kicked in. Maybe there was something wrong. She could have fallen in the shower and hit her head. He needed to find her, see her, talk to her. If he knew any of her neighbors, he'd call them to check on her, but he didn't. So he'd go himself. Anyone in the company who really needed him could call his cell.

He left the house, slamming the door behind him before getting in his car. He peeled out of the driveway, which wasn't like him but seemed appropriate under the circumstances. She didn't live that far away, but the drive seemed to take a lifetime. When he finally got to the apartment complex, he drove in but didn't see her car, so she'd gone somewhere.

Still, he was here and should be thorough. He parked and hurried up the walkway to her door, then knocked loudly. Listening intently, he didn't hear anything from inside, but knocked again anyway, louder this time. It was like raising your voice to someone who didn't speak English, as if a higher decibel level would help them understand what you were saying.

The door next to Olivia's opened and a woman in her late fifties or early sixties came out. She smiled at him, locked her place up and started to walk away. When he rapped again, she stopped and came over.

"Are you looking for Olivia?"

"Yes. I'm her boss. Brady O'Keefe."

"Oh, yes. I've heard about you. She said you were nice-looking, but that doesn't do you justice. You remind me of that actor from the movie *Magic Mike*."

"I don't think I know that one."

"I'm not surprised. It's about male dancers. They're all hunky and seriously ripped. I'm old, not dead." She grinned and held out her hand. "Sally Smith."

"Nice to meet you." So, Olivia had talked about him. That was good, right? "Do you know where she is?"

If the woman thought his not knowing his assistant's whereabouts was strange, she didn't show it. "I don't know. But I saw her leaving pretty early yesterday morning with a suitcase."

"Where was she going?"

"Not a clue. She just said she was taking a vacation and I wished her a good trip." Her blue eyes narrowed now. "Is anything wrong?"

"No." Not a complete lie. There wasn't *any* one thing wrong, it was everything.

"Shouldn't she have told you she was taking a vacation?"

"She probably did." He tried to look as though this was business as usual and hoped he pulled it off. "I have a tendency to tune out everything around me when I'm focused on work."

"Olivia told me that, too. And focus is good." Now there was censure in her voice. "But sometimes you need to stop and smell the coffee."

He'd said something like that to Olivia. "I thought it was roses."

"That, too. Just saying…" She looked at her watch. "I really need to go. An appointment."

"Thanks for your help. It was nice to meet you, Sally."

"Same here. I hope you and Olivia work out your problems."

So much for business as usual.

Brady stood and watched Sally get into her car and drive away. What could he do now? He still needed to talk to Olivia and decided to call her cell again. Again she didn't pick up and he left a message to call.

The next logical step was to see her family. Surely she'd let them know where she'd gone. But it wasn't even noon yet and they worked. Since there wasn't anything he could do right this minute, he went back to the house and tried to accomplish something.

Six hours later he'd done nothing but wear a path in his office carpet and crush the hell out of his orange rubber stress ball.

When the clock said five, he breathed a sigh of relief. Surely someone would be home at the Lawsons' now, since her mother taught at Blackwater Lake Elementary. Again he got in the car and this time went to the neighborhood where he and Olivia had grown up.

There was a car in her parents' driveway and he was pretty sure it belonged to Ann Lawson. He parked at the curb and walked up to the door.

Brady lifted his hand to knock, but it opened before he could and his mother was there with Olivia's mom.

"Brady?" Maureen O'Keefe was obviously surprised. "What are you doing here?"

Just like that, everything went from bad to worse. Getting information from Olivia's mom was an acceptable risk, but his own mother involved in this meant he'd get more than he signed up for. But there was no bluffing his way out of anything now, and he was anxious for answers.

"I came to talk to Mrs. Lawson. Hi," he said to Ann.

"It's nice to see you, Brady. Come in, sweetheart. Your mother was just leaving."

"Not anymore." Maureen backed up so he could come inside. "What's wrong?"

"Why do you go straight to the bad place?"

"Hmm. I'm your mother and I don't think I've ever heard that tone from you before. So I rest my case about something being wrong. You drop by to see me now and then, but never the Lawsons. Clearly something's wrong, and my guess is that it involves Olivia." When he opened his mouth to protest, she held up her hand. "Don't even bother denying the obvious."

The three of them stood in the entryway on the dark

wood floor. A brass chandelier was suspended from the two-story ceiling and a stairway with white spindles was on his right.

Brady dragged his fingers through his hair. "Okay. I should know better than to try and bluff with you."

"Darn right." Maureen nodded emphatically. "It didn't work when you were ten and you're not any better at it now. And I guessed that something happened with you and Olivia, because she left on vacation suddenly and wouldn't say where she was going."

"You don't know where she is?" He looked at Ann.

"She only said she'd be out of town for a while."

"How long?" What he wanted to ask was how long until he could see her, talk to her.

"I couldn't get her to tell me." Ann held up a hand when he opened his mouth to ask more. "And she refused to say where she was going."

That would have been his next question. Instead he asked, "How could she not tell her parents?"

"She said you'd probably come by and give us the third degree. Don't be offended. She also said you have a way of charming things out of people."

"He is persuasive," his mom said. "And charming. Just like his father."

His patience was so thin he expected it to snap any second. And this wasn't a good time to remind him his father was gone and that his mother still missed him. "What does that have to do with anything?"

"Just that the fruit doesn't fall far from the tree." Maureen smiled, some mysterious thing that only she understood.

Ann looked sincerely sorry for him. "Livvie said if we don't know where she is, we can't spill the beans. No matter how persuasive you are."

"If you knew, would you tell me?"

"Probably not." She slid her friend a sorry-'bout-that look. "My daughter is the most levelheaded woman I know. If she doesn't want you to know where she is, I'm positive there's a good reason for that. Even though she won't say what it is." She sighed. "Brady, I love you like a son and would help you if I could. But I wouldn't ever betray Livvie, tempted as I might be. It's a conflict so I'm glad I don't know anything."

"I understand." He slid his fingers into his jeans pockets as he met the other woman's gaze. He really didn't like Olivia out there alone, where he couldn't protect her. He couldn't stand it if anything happened to her. "She's all right, isn't she?"

"Yes. And she promised to check in with her dad or me every day."

"Good." That was something, anyway. "Will you ask her to call me?"

"Of course. But I can't guarantee that she will."

"I know. Just tell her—" What? That he missed her? He was sorry? He'd make it right? How could he do that? "Tell her I'm thinking about her."

Ann smiled. "I will, Brady. It's good to see you."

"Same here."

"But you look like hell," Maureen said.

"Thanks, Mom."

"You're welcome," she said cheerfully. "Come on. We need to go and let Ann relax after a long day at school."

It had been a hell of a day and he was more tired than after a full day when he'd actually worked. "You're right. Bye, Mrs. Lawson."

"Have a good evening, you two," the other woman said.

When the door closed behind them, his mother slid her arm through his. "You're here. It's almost dinnertime. I always make too much. You should stay and eat. What do you think, sweetie?"

"I wouldn't be very good company."

"That's okay. You might want to talk and I'm happy to listen. What's family for?"

"I don't think so, Ma. But thanks."

"Okay. I know not to push."

"Since when?" Her look of mock indignation made him smile, the first and only one all day. And that wasn't normal. Every day with Olivia was filled with teasing and laughter. "It's a good offer, but I'll pass. Thanks anyway."

"Okay, honey." She stood on tiptoe and hugged him hard. "I love you very much."

"Love you, too."

Brady watched her walk safely into the house, then slid into his car. And sat there motionless. For a man who'd always known what he wanted, this was the first time in his life he didn't know what to do, where to go.

He only knew that he couldn't stand to go back to his house without Olivia there.

Chapter Fifteen

Brady drove straight to his sister's house. He stood on the front porch, wondering how she'd managed to keep going after her husband died. The grief had been shattering and was always there in her eyes, yet she'd somehow managed to put one foot in front of the other even though the most important person in her life was no longer there. He hadn't seen Olivia for only two days and he missed her like crazy.

He knocked on the door and prepared to wait because Maggie might be busy with the baby. But in moments she was standing there with the little girl braced on one hip.

"Hi, bro. Come on in."

"Hey. Sorry to drop in unannounced—"

"About that…Mom called."

"What did she tell you?" he asked.

"Everything. Olivia's gone and didn't tell you. Her whereabouts are unknown. True?"

"Yeah."

Maggie smiled sympathetically. "Get in here, Brady."

"Ba-ay!" Danielle held out her arms as she always did.

Brady was happy to take her and grabbed his niece from his sister, then snuggled her close. "That's the best thing that's happened to me all day."

"I'm sorry. I really am." Then Maggie shook her head disapprovingly. "But you brought this on yourself."

The little girl in his arms was running her hands over the scruff of whiskers on his face, then looked at her palms questioningly.

"Excuse me," he said. "I could have sworn you just said this is my fault."

"It is."

"How do you figure that? You're the one who helped her pull off a lie."

"And I'd do it again." His sister crossed her arms over her chest.

"Did we have the same parents?" Brady asked. When his niece squirmed and pressed her tiny, chubby hands against his chest, he set her gently on the colorful braided rug in the living room. Instantly she sat and picked up a stuffed doll from underneath the coffee table. "Because my mother and father taught me that it was wrong to deceive someone."

"Sometimes you have to do the wrong thing for the right reason." She nodded her head sagely.

"Now you sound like Confucius. Or Yoda."

"My parents taught me not to call people names."

"Don't throw my words back at me." He was in no mood for anything other than a straightforward answer. "I'm your own flesh and blood. Why would you encourage Olivia to lie to me?"

"Because you needed a good shaking up."

"What?" He stared at her. "Why would you say that? I was just fine, thank you very much."

"I'll give you an answer, but first I have a question." Before waiting for the okay, she said, "What happened between you and Olivia?"

"Nothing." The word nearly stuck in his throat and he couldn't quite meet his sister's inquiring gaze.

"Now *you're* lying." She turned away. "Do you want a beer or a glass of wine?"

"Wait a minute." He followed her toward the kitchen. "First you call me a liar and now you're being nice?"

"Of course." She smiled wickedly. "What are little sisters for? Try to keep up."

"Beer." He shook his head to clear it.

"Okay, then." She opened the refrigerator and pulled out a longneck amber bottle, then handed it to him to twist off the top.

Danielle toddled into the room after them and held out the soft, cuddly doll. "Ba-ay?"

"Thank you, sweetheart." He took it from her and stared at the well-used toy. "This is the kind of woman I can handle. Does what you tell her. Never lies about a boyfriend. Always there when you need her." His niece held up her arms and was moving her fingers in a way that meant *give me back my doll.* "Easy come, easy go," he said, holding it out for her.

Maggie had poured herself a glass of red wine. "I have chicken in the oven. Want to stay for dinner?"

"Really? You'd feed your brother, a name-calling, lie-telling weasel who needs a shaking up?"

"Yes," she said empathetically. "It's the least I can do."

"You got that right. And thanks. I'd like that."

She glanced at the timer on the stove. "I just put it in, so we won't be eating for a while." There was an evil gleam in her eyes. "That will give us a chance to talk."

She breezed past him and he looked heavenward because divine intervention for this conversation would be incredibly helpful. He followed his niece back into the living room, where she plopped herself on the floor and happily chattered away in a language no one else, with the possible exception of her mother, could understand.

When Maggie was settled in her chair, he sat at a right angle to her on the couch. "Okay, Brady, tell me what you did."

"Really?" He blinked at her. "Olivia disappeared. Why am I the bad guy?"

"Oh, please. This is me." She looked at him as if he was the most pathetic human being on the face of the planet. "This behavior is uncharacteristic for Olivia. She's organized and responsible. She'd never take off without notifying work and especially without telling her parents where she'd gone. Clearly she doesn't want to be found."

"How do you know all this?" They stared at each other for several moments before he realized it was a stupid question. Maggie had already told him she'd talked to their mother.

"So what made her go?" Maggie persisted.

"You're not giving up on this, are you?" Brady wasn't really asking. He took a drink of his beer, then set it on the coaster beside him. "Okay. Just remember you made me. Because it's really bad form. A gentleman doesn't kiss and tell—"

Maggie's eyes widened and she nearly choked on her wine. "You had sex with Olivia."

He angled his head toward the toddler. "Little ears. Language."

"She's not even two yet. She doesn't know what sex

means." Maggie set her wineglass down on the coffee table. "Finally! You and Olivia did the wild thing."

Wild wasn't the way Brady remembered it. Being that close to her had been intimate and sexy and powerfully moving. It was a moment, with a capital *M.* And now everything was messed up.

"Yes," he admitted. "Saturday night after the employee weekend officially ended, I took her to my suite at Blackwater Lake Lodge and we—"

"Did the horizontal hokeypokey."

"Maggie—" His voice rose and the baby stopped playing to stare at him wide-eyed. "Sorry, sweetheart. Your mom is exasperating."

"One of my best qualities," she bragged. "What I don't get is why you're so peeved. Obviously you two have some chemistry going on."

Brady couldn't deny that. It was by turns the best and worst night of his life. Now he was two parts miserable and one part really ticked off.

"I want to unring that bell and I can't. Everything has changed and I want it back the way it was. Damn it—"

"Language. Little ears," she said, pointing at the baby, who looked up. "Tone makes her pay attention and I'd prefer she not blurt that out at next week's play group. If she does, I'm blaming it on you."

"Might as well add that to my list of sins." He dragged his fingers through his hair. "I really messed up, Mags."

"Oh, Brady." She leaned forward and put her hand on his arm. "I'm sorry I teased. I've never seen you like this. What happened?"

"She confessed all to me about Leonard, told me that she'd made him up. Then she admitted why, that it was to help her stick to her guns and leave the company." In for a penny, in for a pound. Might as well give her the whole truth. "She said she's in love with me and has been for a long time."

"Hip, hip, hooray and hallelujah. It's about doggone time." Maggie's smile faltered when she noticed he wasn't feeling the joy. "What did you say to her?"

"Nothing. I was stunned." Did he look as miserable as he felt? It was probably best not to reveal that this conversation had taken place in bed while they were naked. But he would never forget the hopeless, unhappy expression on Olivia's face before she'd grabbed her clothes and left. He would never forgive himself and hated that he was responsible for making her look that way. "The next thing I knew she'd walked out."

"You didn't go after her?" There was a note of astonishment in his sister's voice.

"I thought she needed space. I didn't know what to say to her."

Maggie pressed her lips together, clearly disapproving. "*This* is why you needed a shaking up. And that's why I played my part in Olivia's lie."

"You were manipulating me."

"That's kind of a harsh word," Maggie said. "Let's call it helping you see the light."

"About?" He stared at her. "What the heck are you saying?"

Maggie tapped her lip thoughtfully. "More importantly, what are you going to do about Olivia?"

"Even if I wanted to—"

"Oh, you do." His sister smiled knowingly. "Otherwise you wouldn't have gone to her parents. But please feel free to continue digging yourself in deeper."

"I repeat, even if I wanted to, there's nothing I can do because I don't know where she is."

"There are so many things wrong with that statement I don't even know where to begin."

"Give it a try, because I don't have a clue."

"That's pretty clear." She drew in a deep breath. "Let's start with this. You're a computer genius, Brady. If you can't find her, she can't be found."

He hated to admit it, but Maggie was right. He should have thought of that, and would have if he hadn't been thrown off balance by everything. It was a state that had started when Olivia got his attention with a boyfriend that wasn't even real.

"I knew that," he said sheepishly.

"Here's the thing…I love you and want to see you happy. The last thing I want is for you to end up unloved and alone. For years you've been pushing away anyone who had even the slightest chance of getting close to you." She met his gaze. "Then you hired Olivia and I thought given enough time you'd realize that the two of you are perfect for each other."

"You think?"

"Duh," she said. "But you kept the cone of detachment firmly in place until I wanted to shake you myself. I wanted to tell you that Dad would be really upset and angry if you passed up a chance at love, especially because of him. He and Mom loved each other so much. You know as well as I do that from the day she lost him she always said she'd rather have had one day with him than not to have been with him at all. And since I'm speaking my mind here, it's time to stop punishing yourself for not dying in that accident with Henry."

"Olivia said the same thing."

Maggie smiled and tapped her temple. "Great minds…"

"Uh-huh."

"We'll talk about that later. The thing is, when Olivia

told me about the lie, it was obvious that you'd finally noticed her in a different way. Of course I helped her. And you."

"It doesn't feel like it. Feels like hell," he grumbled.

He missed Olivia in every way it was possible to miss a woman. Nothing was right—and he somehow knew that without her it never would be again.

"Only you can fix this," Maggie said. "The ball is in your court, Brady. Tell her what's in your heart. She's not a mind reader. Put up or shut up."

"I can't shut up. I love her." Lightning didn't strike and the earth didn't shift on its axis. But suddenly the truth of his feelings for Olivia was as vivid and clear as a Montana sky the day after a storm.

Maggie grinned as if he was her star pupil. "Don't tell me. Tell her."

"Right after I find her," he agreed.

Olivia had hoped being in Miami Beach would make her forget she was completely miserable. There were palm trees and the beautiful Atlantic Ocean, and the city hummed with excitement. She was stretched out on a luxurious beach towel with fine grains of sand between her toes as the balmy breeze blew over her. Winter in Montana was far away and the sound of waves lapping on the shore should have been peaceful, but it wasn't.

In reality, she was warm on the outside and freezing inside. This was her fourth day and so far there was no sign of that changing any time soon.

She fished her phone from her beach bag and checked the display. The first day she hadn't been at work, Brady had called her repeatedly. His voice mails had grown increasingly frustrated and angry. Then he'd stopped trying to reach her. When she looked now, the words *zero messages* mocked her. Wow, he'd gotten over her really fast.

"I'm such a loser."

The beach was filled with people, most of them probably taking a break from cold weather, which had been her plan as well. But she'd brought winter along in her heart.

At the start of the new year, it had seemed critically important to get away from Brady in order to have a life. Now that she was away, the flaws in the plan were immediately apparent. She missed him more than she'd thought possible. Maybe it would be better to apologize, ask for her job back and stay in Blackwater Lake. Although she'd insisted he hire her replacement, so she wasn't sure how it would work. Maybe there would be a job when the corporate headquarters was completed. She could find something to tide herself over and wait. Wouldn't it be better to at least see him every day, even if he couldn't love her? Friendship could work, right?

A shadow fell over her but didn't move on. She was too crabby for this, crabby enough to ask the inconsiderate bozo to get the heck out of her sun. When she finally looked up, she recognized the inconsiderate bozo.

"Brady?" Maybe it was just because she'd been thinking about him. Or had she been out in the sun too long?

"Hi, Liv." Sure sounded like his voice.

He had on cargo shorts, a white T-shirt and aviator sunglasses that hid his eyes. A beach towel identical to the one she'd borrowed from her hotel was rolled up under his arm. "I like your bikini."

Oh, God. She'd never pictured herself in a two-piece bathing suit for this conversation. Even a tasteful but flattering one-piece tank would have been better, although not especially professional or appropriate for Montana in the waning weeks of winter.

"Do you need sunscreen on your back?" he asked.

That really didn't seem important at this particular moment, so she ignored the offer. "How did you find me?"

"Really?" His tone dripped with the infamous O'Keefe confidence. "This is me."

So he'd used his computer skills to track her down. Did that mean he cared just a little?

She expected a cocky grin and was surprised when there wasn't one. "Are you taking a break from winter? Or, since technically I still had one more week to work, did you come to fire me in person?"

"Neither."

"Then I don't understand."

"Do you mind if I sit?"

"I don't own the beach. Suit yourself." Where did that attitude come from? She might look relaxed on the outside, but inside she was a quivering bundle of nerves and pounding heart.

Without comment he arranged his towel next to hers. She faced the ocean and he stretched out beside her with his back to the waves. She sat up and their thighs brushed, creating a man-made heat that had nothing to do with the sun. He was close enough to kiss her. If he wanted.

"Well?" she said. "I didn't expect you to go to so much trouble."

"Funny thing about expectations." He rested a forearm on his raised knee. "I never expected you to disappear without a word."

"There was nothing left to say." The humiliation of that night was still fresh. After she'd declared her years-long love for him, he hadn't responded. If there was a God in heaven, she would never go through an experience like that ever again.

"You're wrong about that. I never had my say. You

dumped all your feelings on me, then took off before I had a chance to process anything."

"My bad. It never occurred to me that my words were encrypted." Funny thing about embarrassment. It tended to make her resentful and defensive—and just a tad sarcastic. "I forgot the legendary Brady brain needed to organize and filter data through microchips and circuit boards. That's your personal default operating system."

"I don't do knee-jerk reactions."

"That's just an excuse. We've known each other for years. It seems a sufficient amount of time to know how you feel. At least for me."

"Your life experience lets you be more open to that sort of thing. Mine was different." He looked down for a moment. "You like to joke that when I found computers, I found a friend, the subtext being that I don't have a heart. Because I do. Computers are safer than people. They're less messy and there's always a way to fix a broken one. I tend to compartmentalize everything. Even more after losing my father and best friend. It hurt a lot, so I put the people in my life into manageable subsets. I love my family and there's nothing I can do to change that. Even if I could I wouldn't."

Olivia couldn't see his eyes, but the rest of his body spoke loud and clear about his inner conflict. The way his mouth pulled tight. The muscle jerking in his jaw. His fingers clenching into a fist. All of it told her he was voluntarily opening up, revealing the depth of his pain. She was afraid to say anything and stop him. Break the spell. So she watched and waited and held her breath.

"I consciously made the choice not to let anyone else get close."

"Including me." It had to be said and wasn't a question.

"Especially you." He drew in a shuddering breath. "I

put you in the business category. Work only. That made you off-limits personally."

"I see."

"No, you don't." He must have heard the hurt in her voice, because there was frustration in his. "When I interviewed you for my executive assistant, you were all grown up and pretty as a picture. You're smart and funny and weren't afraid to tell me when I was full of it. You kept me grounded and instinctively I knew you could be more if I wasn't careful."

"So you were careful and kept me in my subset."

"I had to. Otherwise there'd have been more to lose and I'd already lost enough. But day after day you were there—sweet, sassy, telling it like it is. I just couldn't keep you out no matter how hard I tried."

"Why?" She really wanted to know.

"You brought me out of the shadows. And keeping it real, I have to say the light wasn't comfortable at first—"

"You're a vampire?"

That got a small smile. "In a way. Hard knocks sucked the will to try right out of me. My goal was to keep everything status quo. You came to work every day and I could see you. As long as it stayed business, nothing could change. I couldn't lose."

"So what happened?"

"In a word?" He slid his sunglasses to the top of his head and met her gaze. "Leonard."

"But he wasn't real," she protested.

"I didn't know that at first. The idea of you leaving me was unacceptable and despite what you think, it wasn't about replacing you. On some level that I tried very hard not to acknowledge, I knew you were irreplaceable. Since I'm groveling here, I might as well go for broke." He blew out a breath. "I was jealous."

"Really?"

"Insane with it."

Happiness filled her to overflowing. This had seemed like the wrong time and place for a bare-your-soul talk. It was so very public. They were on a beach where children dug in the sand and played tag with the surf. But there were breezes and an endless blue sky overhead. It was the absolutely perfect place to talk about the past, present, future.

She was pretty sure she knew where he was headed with this, but it was as important for him to get the words out as it was for her to hear them. Computers and technology were all well and good in their place but would never be a substitute for human interaction, which he was pretty rusty at. That wasn't going to fly now. No more hiding in the shadows for him.

"Go on. I'm listening," she said.

He reached over and loosely took her fingers in his. "I need you, Liv. I didn't know how much until I thought I'd lost you to another guy. And I realized something else."

"Oh?"

"Standing on the sidelines isn't living. I'd rather have one day with you than a lifetime alone."

"Better to have loved and lost than never to have loved at all?"

"Something like that. People leave us for reasons we can't do anything about. I realized when you left me that I'm being stupid not to try."

"We both know you're not stupid," she said.

"I hope you still feel that way, because I'm putting it all on the line here." He took her hand more securely and met her gaze. "You can leave me, but I'll just track you down. And we both know I can do it."

"Should I be afraid?" she teased.

"When I say track, I don't mean in a creepy, stalker kind of way."

"Then what kind of way are you talking?" No getting off the hook. She'd waited too long to hear him say this.

"I'm talking love. As in I love you. I want to marry you and have a family with you." He brushed his thumb over her knuckles. "But make no mistake. I will not be a pretend boyfriend. I'm talking husband. And I am the boss."

"At work," she agreed. "At home, that's a different story. How about a fifty-fifty partnership?"

"Okay, I'm not very good at this kind of stuff so I need it spelled out. Did you just say what I think you did?"

With her index finger she smoothed out the sand and drew a heart. Inside it she wrote *I love you.*

"In case that's not spelled out clearly enough for you, I'll say it. I love you, Brady O'Keefe. I fell for you long before you were my boss and this feels like a dream come true."

"So you'll marry me?"

"Nothing would make me happier." She smiled. "Now I'd appreciate it if you'd kiss me."

"Pretty bossy, aren't you?" He moved closer and his mouth was a whisper from hers when he said, "That works for me."

And then, right there on a public beach in front of everyone, Brady O'Keefe kissed her for a very, very long time.

* * * * *

COMING NEXT MONTH FROM

H HARLEQUIN®

SPECIAL EDITION

Available April 15, 2014

#2329 THE PRINCE'S CINDERELLA BRIDE
The Bravo Royales • by Christine Rimmer
Lani Vasquez cherishes her role as nanny to the Montedoran royal children—particularly since it offers proximity to her good friend, the handsome Prince Maximilian. Max has grieved his lost wife for years, but this Prince Charming is ready for the next chapter of his love story—and his Cinderella is right under his nose.

#2330 FALLING FOR FORTUNE
The Fortunes of Texas: Welcome to Horseback Hollow
by Nancy Robards Thompson
Christopher Fortune has gladly embraced the wealth and power of his newfound family name. But not everyone's as impressed by the Fortune legacy. His new coworker, Kinsley Aaron, worked for everything she ever got, and Chris's newly entitled attitude rubs her the wrong way. Now Chris will have to earn Kinsley's love—and his Fortune fairy-tale ending....

#2331 THE HUSBAND LIST
Rx for Love • by Cindy Kirk
Great job? Check. Hunky hubby? Not so much. Dr. Mitzi Sanchez has her life just where she wants it—except for the husband she's always dreamed of. She creates a checklist for her perfect man—but she insists pilot Keenan McGregor isn't it. With a bit of luck, Keenan might blow Mitzi's expectations sky-high....

#2332 HEALED WITH A KISS
Bride Mountain • by Gina Wilkins
Both burned by love, wedding planner Alexis Mosley and innkeeper Logan Carmichael aren't looking for anything serious when they plunge into a passionate affair. Little by little, though, what starts as a no-strings-attached fling evolves into something much deeper. Can they heal their emotional wounds to start afresh, or will the ghosts of relationships past haunt them forever?

#2333 GROOMED FOR LOVE
Sweet Springs, Texas • by Helen R. Myers
Due to her declining sight, Rylie Quinn abandoned her dreams of becoming a veterinarian and moved to Sweet Springs, Texas, as an animal groomer. She just wants to get on with her life—something that irritating attorney Noah Prescott won't allow her to do. He's determined to dig up Rylie's past, and, as he and Rylie butt heads, true love might just rear its own.

#2334 THE BACHELOR DOCTOR'S BRIDE
The Doctors MacDowell • by Caro Carson
Bright, free-spirited and bubbly, Diana Connor gets under detached cardiologist Quinn MacDowell's skin...and not in a way he'd care to admit. When the two are forced to work together at a field clinic, Quinn begins to see just how caring Diana is and how well she interacts with patients. This heart doctor might just need a bit of Diana's medicine for himself....

————————

HSECNM0414

REQUEST YOUR FREE BOOKS!
2 FREE NOVELS PLUS 2 FREE GIFTS!

♥ HARLEQUIN®

SPECIAL EDITION
Life, Love & Family

YES! Please send me 2 FREE Harlequin® Special Edition novels and my 2 FREE gifts (gifts are worth about $10). After receiving them, if I don't wish to receive any more books, I can return the shipping statement marked "cancel." If I don't cancel, I will receive 6 brand-new novels every month and be billed just $4.74 per book in the U.S. or $5.24 per book in Canada. That's a savings of at least 14% off the cover price! It's quite a bargain! Shipping and handling is just 50¢ per book in the U.S. and 75¢ per book in Canada.* I understand that accepting the 2 free books and gifts places me under no obligation to buy anything. I can always return a shipment and cancel at any time. Even if I never buy another book, the two free books and gifts are mine to keep forever.

235/335 HDN F45Y

Name	(PLEASE PRINT)

Address		Apt. #

City	State/Prov.	Zip/Postal Code

Signature (if under 18, a parent or guardian must sign)

Mail to the **Harlequin® Reader Service:**
IN U.S.A.: P.O. Box 1867, Buffalo, NY 14240-1867
IN CANADA: P.O. Box 609, Fort Erie, Ontario L2A 5X3

Want to try two free books from another line?
Call 1-800-873-8635 or visit www.ReaderService.com.

* Terms and prices subject to change without notice. Prices do not include applicable taxes. Sales tax applicable in N.Y. Canadian residents will be charged applicable taxes. Offer not valid in Quebec. This offer is limited to one order per household. Not valid for current subscribers to Harlequin Special Edition books. All orders subject to credit approval. Credit or debit balances in a customer's account(s) may be offset by any other outstanding balance owed by or to the customer. Please allow 4 to 6 weeks for delivery. Offer available while quantities last.

Your Privacy—The Harlequin® Reader Service is committed to protecting your privacy. Our Privacy Policy is available online at www.ReaderService.com or upon request from the Harlequin Reader Service.

We make a portion of our mailing list available to reputable third parties that offer products we believe may interest you. If you prefer that we not exchange your name with third parties, or if you wish to clarify or modify your communication preferences, please visit us at www.ReaderService.com/consumerchoice or write to us at Harlequin Reader Service Preference Service, P.O. Box 9062, Buffalo, NY 14269. Include your complete name and address.

HSE13R

SPECIAL EXCERPT FROM

H HARLEQUIN®

SPECIAL EDITION

*Lani Vasquez is a nanny to the royal children of
Montedoro...and nothing more, or so she thinks.
But widower Prince Maximilian Bravo-Calabretti
hasn't forgotten their single passionate encounter.
Can the handsome prince and the alluring au pair turn
one night into forever? Or will their love turn Lani into a
pumpkin at the stroke of midnight?*

***

He was fresh out of new tactics and had no clue how to get her to let down her guard. Plus he had a very strong feeling that he'd pushed her as far as she would go for now. This was looking to be an extended campaign. He didn't like that, but if it was the only way to finally reach her, so be it. "I'll be seeing you in the library—where you will no longer scuttle away every time I get near you."

A hint of the old humor flashed in her eyes. "I never scuttle."

"Scamper? Dart? Dash?"

"Stop it." Her mouth twitched. A good sign, he told himself. "Promise me you won't run off the next time we meet."

The spark of humor winked out. "I just don't like this."

"You've already said that. I'm going to show you there's nothing to be afraid of. Do we have an understanding?"

"Oh, Max..."

"Say yes."

And finally, she gave in and said the words he needed to hear. "Yes. I'll, um, look forward to seeing you."

He didn't believe her. How could he believe her when she sounded so grim, when that mouth he wanted beneath his own was twisted with resignation? He didn't believe her, and he almost wished he could give her what she said she wanted, let her go, say goodbye. He almost wished he could *not* care.

But he'd had so many years of not caring. Years and years when he'd told himself that not caring was for the best.

And then the small, dark-haired woman in front of him changed everything.

***

Enjoy this sneak peek from Christine Rimmer's
THE PRINCE'S CINDERELLA BRIDE,
the latest installment in her Harlequin® Special Edition
miniseries **THE BRAVO ROYALES,** *on sale May 2014!*

Coming in May 2014

HEALED WITH A KISS
by reader-favorite author
Gina Wilkins

Both burned by love, wedding planner Alexis Mosley
and innkeeper Logan Carmichael aren't looking for
anything serious when they plunge into a passionate
affair. Little by little, though, what starts as a
no-strings-attached fling evolves into something
much deeper. Can they heal their emotional wounds
to start afresh, or will the ghosts of relationships past
haunt them forever?

*Don't miss the third edition of the
Bride Mountain trilogy!*

Available now from the
Bride Mountain trilogy by Gina Wilkins:

*MATCHED BY MOONLIGHT
A PROPOSAL AT THE WEDDING*

HARLEQUIN®

SPECIAL EDITION

Life, Love and Family

Coming in May 2014 from
Cindy Kirk

THE HUSBAND LIST

Great job? Check. Hunky hubby? Not so much.
Dr. Mitzi Sanchez has her life just where she wants
it—except for the husband she's always dreamed
of. She creates a checklist for her perfect man—but
she insists pilot Keenan McGregor isn't it. With a
bit of luck, Keenan might blow Mitzi's expectations
sky-high….

*Look for the latest in the **Rx for Love** miniseries
from Harlequin® Special Edition®,
wherever books and ebooks are sold!*

HSE65813